THE HIDDEN HEART

BY LINDSAY MCKENNA

Blue Turtle Publishing

Praise for Lindsay McKenna

"A treasure of a book . . . highly recommended reading that everyone will enjoy and learn from."

—Chief Michael Jaco, US Navy SEAL, retired, on Breaking Point

"Readers will root for this complex heroine, scarred both inside and out, and hope she finds peace with her steadfast and loving hero. Rife with realistic conflict and spiced with danger, this is a worthy page-turner."

—BookPage.com on Taking Fire
March 2015 Top Pick in Romance

". . . is fast-paced romantic suspense that renders a beautiful love story, start to finish. McKenna's writing is flawless, and her story line fully absorbing. More, please."

—Annalisa Pesek, Library Journal on Taking Fire

"Ms. McKenna masterfully blends the two different paces to convey a beautiful saga about love, trust, patience and having faith in each other."

—Fresh Fiction on Never Surrender

"Genuine and moving, this romantic story set in the complex world of military ops grabs at the heart."

—RT Book Reviews on Risk Taker

"McKenna does a beautiful job of illustrating difficult topics through the development of well-formed, sympathetic characters."

—Publisher's Weekly (starred review) on Wolf Haven
One of the Best Books of 2014, Publisher's Weekly

"McKenna delivers a story that is raw and heartfelt. The relationship between Kell and Leah is both passionate and tender. Kell is the hero every woman wants, and McKenna employs skill and empathy to craft a physically and emotionally abused character in Leah. Using tension and steady pacing, McKenna is adept at expressing growing, tender love in the midst of high stakes danger."

—RT Book Reviews on Taking Fire

"Her military background lends authenticity to this outstanding tale, and readers will fall in love with the upstanding hero and his fierce determination to save the woman he loves.

—Publishers Weekly (starred review) on Never Surrender
One of the Best Books of 2014, Publisher's Weekly

"Readers will find this addition to the Shadow Warriors series full of intensity and action-packed romance. There is great chemistry between the characters and tremendous realism, making Breaking Point a great read."

—RT Book Reviews

"This sequel to Risk Taker is an action-packed, compelling story, and the sizzling chemistry between Ethan and Sarah makes this a good read."

—RT Book Reviews on Degree of Risk

"McKenna elicits tears, laughter, fist-pumping triumph, and most all, a desire for the next tale in this powerful series."

—Publishers Weekly (starred review) on Running Fire

"McKenna's military experience shines through in this moving tale . . . McKenna (High Country Rebel) skillfully takes readers on an emotional journey into modern warfare and two people's hearts."

—Publisher's Weekly on Down Range

"Lindsay McKenna has proven that she knows what she's doing when it comes to these military action/romance books."

—Terry Lynn, Amazon on Zone of Fire.

"At no time do you want to put your book down and come back to it later! Last Chance is a well written, fast paced, short (remember that) story that will please any military romance reader!"

—LBDDiaries, Amazon on Last Chance.

Available from
Lindsay McKenna

Blue Turtle Publishing

DELOS

Last Chance, prologue novella to Nowhere to Hide
Nowhere to Hide, Book 1
Tangled Pursuit, Book 2
Forged in Fire, Book 3

2016

Broken Dreams, Book 4
Blind Sided, BN2
Secret Dream, B1B novella, epilogue to Nowhere to
Hide
Hold On, Book 5
Hold Me, 5B1, sequel to Hold On
Unbound Pursuit, 2B1 novella, epilogue to Tangled
Pursuit
Secrets, 2B2 novella, sequel to Unbound Pursuit, 2B1

2017

Snowflake's Gift, Book 6
Never Enough, 3B1, novella, sequel to Forged in Fire
Dream of Me, 4B1, novella, sequel to Broken Dreams
Trapped, Book 7
Taking a Chance 7B1, novella, sequel to Trapped
The Hidden Heart, 7B2, novella, sequel to Taking A
Chance

Harlequin/HQN/Harlequin Romantic Suspense

SHADOW WARRIORS
Danger Close
Down Range
Risk Taker
Degree of Risk
Breaking Point
Never Surrender
Zone of Fire
Taking Fire
On Fire
Running Fire

THE WYOMING SERIES
Shadows From The Past
Deadly Identity
Deadly Silence
The Last Cowboy
The Wrangler
The Defender
The Loner
High Country Rebel
Wolf Haven
Night Hawk
Out Rider

WIND RIVER VALLEY SERIES, Kensington

2016
Wind River Wrangler
Wind River Rancher

2017
Wind River Cowboy
Christmas with my Cowboy
Wrangler's Challenge

The Hidden Heart

Dedication

To my many global readers: You're the greatest! Thank you for reading my stories and I hope it gives you a 'time out' from this chaotic world of ours for at least a few hours!

Dear Reader,

The Hidden Heart is the spin-off sequel novella 7B2 to *Trapped*, Book 7 and *Taking A Chance*, 7B1. The two main characters you met earlier, Artemis agent and ex-SEAL, Tyler Hutton, and Cara Montero, were introduced in the above two books. Now, this is THEIR story! I love being able to write about secondary characters and be able to tell their story, as well.

Ali's younger sister, Cara, was kidnapped off the streets of Tucson, Arizona and whisked across the Mexican border to become a sex slave. When Cara is captured, Ali will do anything to help rescue her sister from the hands of this drug lord. Ram, his team, and Ali are able to rescue Cara and bring her back home, where *The Hidden Heart* begins.

Can Cara heal from her kidnapping and go back to the life as a kindergarten teacher that she loves so much? When Ram, and then Ali, leave for Artemis, she feels abandoned in the middle of her healing progress. Artemis assigns Tyler Hutton to continue as her bodyguard while she regains her strength and purpose once more. Will they find how much they were drawn to one another back then, but unable to act upon it?

This is the story of Cara learning to trust. So much was taken away from her. The blunt emotional trauma of being a kidnap victim about to be sold as a sex slave to an unknown buyer in

Asia, tore her world apart. She's home now, but the reverberations of such imprisonment and trauma needs to be worked through. Sometimes, just knowing a person's past helps the other person put it into proper understanding. Cara and Tyler have their work cut out for them. Leave a traumatic past behind? Have the courage to trust one another? Can love take root, then?

I hope you enjoy their story!

Thank you for purchasing this book. I truly hope you enjoy it. If it leaves you with warm fuzzies, please think about writing a review on it for me. Reviews are VERY important and helpful in bringing new readers to my series. If you would love to review but never have, just get a hold of me at docbones224@earthlink.net and I'll send you my little article on how to write a dynamite review! Thank you!

CHAPTER 1

November

"GRAB HER!"

"Oh, no!" Cara Montero groaned as she watched one of Emilio Azarola's drug soldiers grab one of her fellow prisoners, blonde, attractive Inga, in the large outdoor cage.

Cara watched mutely, still unable to believe she was actually living this nightmare. Two weeks ago, three drug dealers who had been driving around looking for women to kidnap to be sold as sex slaves overseas, had dragged her off the streets of Tucson.

The day had been warm, bright, and sunny, and people were out in numbers enjoying the fine weather and the local shops and bistros. No one expected to be snatched in broad daylight from the streets of a major city.

And then the men had spotted Cara, innocently walking down the street, just blocks from her home. They screeched to a halt, grabbed her off the sidewalk, and pushed her into the van. Stunned, unable to fathom what was happening, she had been wrestled to the floor by two masked men, held down, and injected with a drug that rendered her unconscious.

Then she had been driven to a two-story villa deep in the mountains of Sonora, Mexico. Cara still didn't know where she was except for fragments of conversation she'd heard from the soldiers who spoke Spanish. She knew the men reported to a drug dealer named Emilio Azarola, but that was all. The three German tourists in the cage with her spoke a little English, enough that they could talk stiltedly between themselves.

She knew her gentle, loving parents, Mary and Diego Montero, must be frantic not knowing what had happened to their daughter and every day Cara prayed that someone would rescue her. The day after her abduction, three captured German tourists had joined her in her cell. The four women had bonded in desperation, despite their language barrier.

Now, Inga screamed as one of the men grabbed her by the arm, dragging her toward the tall, rusty iron door, now open, where two more armed soldiers stood. She tried resisting, but the more she struggled, the more the men laughed. Finally, one of them cursed her in Spanish and slapped her hard, knocking her to the ground. She lay there, crumpled, as the other women gasped and shrank back, knowing what was coming next.

Cara pressed her hand across her mouth to stop from screaming, and watched as the woman was jerked upward, shakily standing barefoot before her gloating captors. The men had taken the women's shoes away so they couldn't escape. But where would they go? Deep mountain forest surrounded the area for as far as she could see. *Dios*, she wished she knew how far they were to the US border!

Inga's tormentor pushed her toward the opened villa door as the other men laughed, rubbed their crotches, and grinned at each other. Yes, they were going to rape Inga. *Again*.

Cara turned away, unable to watch. She couldn't bear to see the horror on Inga's face, her tears, and then hear her wild-animal screams. Every morning after breakfast, a group of soldiers came out and grabbed one of the three women. For some reason, they had spared Cara, but she knew her time would come.

She gulped, her mouth filled with a bitter taste, her stomach roiling with nausea. Cara felt almost out of body as the cell door was once more slammed shut, a heavy chain and padlock keeping them prisoner. Hannah and Eva, the other two women, were thirty-five and forty-five, respectively. They were huddled together, sobbing, hot tears rolling down their cheeks—one woman's pain belonged to all of them.

The worst news, which the drug soldiers enjoyed telling them daily, was that the women were now sex slaves and would be driven over to Baja, Mexico. There, they would board a container ship in Puerto Nuevo, bound for Asia, that was due to arrive in another week. Azarola had already sold all four of them after taking humiliating pictures of them stripped naked, their genitals prominently exposed.

Although Cara had not been raped, she was terrified that one morning, after choking down her meal, they would grab her and haul her off to the villa where unspeakable sexual acts had been committed upon her cellmates. They often spent three to four hours being passed around between ten to twenty drug soldiers for their sick pleasure.

Yesterday, the men had hauled Hannah and Eva out of the enclosure. This morning the women were still in shock from yesterday's rape and assault, shivering uncontrollably. All three of them were white, with beautiful blonde or red hair, and blue eyes.

In contrast, Cara was half Yaqui Indian through her mother and half Mexican through her father. She had golden skin, black hair, and brown eyes. Clearly, these soldiers, some of whom came from overseas—including Russia—

preferred the statuesque German women. Could it be that her brown skin was saving her from the same degradation as her companions? Or maybe the soldiers had some special selection she didn't know about? If only she knew!

Cara's stomach revolted and she vomited up what little food she had eaten. Arising, she went to one of two large, black rubber water buckets. Kneeling down, she cupped the warm water, and washed the awful taste from her mouth.

She stared over at the villa, a white limestone structure, that looked more like a fancy French castle. There were always men on watch carrying AK-47s. They wore Kevlar vests and their heads were shaved bare. Their job was obviously security, and they made a regular circuit around the huge, walled courtyard.

Cara slowly got to her feet again and went back to where Hannah and Eva stood, clinging to one another.

There was a more protected area at the back of the cell where they all slept on blankets thrown to them by the soldiers. Two pots in the cell were for latrine use and she could smell the urine as the mild breeze shifted through their enclosure. She stood behind the other women and wrapped her arms around their trembling shoulders.

Right now, language was unnecessary—there were no words to give them comfort. They were at the mercy of Azarola's monsters, men who enjoyed hurting them, and hardened even more when the women screamed and cried. Cara rested her head against Eva's filthy blonde curls, and held her with all her strength, letting her know she cared. That was all she could do.

Cara had been told that she was going to a special buyer in Singapore, one who had paid a large sum for her. *What did that mean?* Every day she kicked herself for not having paid more attention to the media's warnings about sex trafficking—but these things happened to other women, surely not her, a kindergarten school-teacher!

She had always been the gentle child, while her older sister by two years, Aliyana, was strong, confident, and a born leader. Ali had gone into the Marine Corps, and was one of the few women to graduate from its world-class sniper school. She had already saved countless lives with her military skills. Now, she was out of the Marines and working for the CIA. Obviously, that was all she could tell her family, since her work was top secret. Cara didn't even know where Ali was right now.

Oh, Lady of Guadalupe! Cara prayed daily to all the saints she could think of. *Help us! Dios, please help us!*

Hannah and Eva continued to sob softly, and Cara tried to hold them tighter, but she was weak from throwing up most of her meals. For some reason, her companions never threw up, which made her feel more vulnerable. She had always been sensitive to the pain of others.

Every day, a guard would bring out two buckets of warm water, one for washing and one for rinsing. But unlike the others, Cara was given a ginger scented shampoo and conditioner to wash her hair. Then, she would be taken to another area within the outer grounds, and given a warm shower with soap and a white, fluffy towel to dry off with behind the privacy of a closed opaque curtain. Still, she hated the new, fear-drenched odor she emitted, and the dirt on her flesh from living in squalor.

Why did the soldiers treat her differently? They never manhandled her as they did her three friends. No one tried to touch her, pinch her, or rub her breasts and behind—the other women had terrible bruises on their arms and around their necks.

The four women found that two buckets of water left little to wash their faces and hands—let alone wash their hair—and they learned quickly that the buckets of water set inside their cage should be used only for drinking.

Cara usually had beautiful, coal black hair with blue highlights when the sun hit it just right. It was halfway down her back, and her mother had taught her at a young age to use olive oil to keep it sleek. Every Saturday, she would wrap her thick, slightly curled hair, in a white towel while the oil seeped into her strands. When she washed it an hour later, it would gleam, looking impossibly beautiful.

One soldier had told her at the shower facility that she was special, which apparently meant she would get better treatment than the other women. The man in Singapore who had bought her wanted her skin in perfect condition, unbruised, and her hair and body clean. Cara was afraid to ask the soldier more, but because he seemed to be in a good mood, she did. He said it was because even though she was twenty-six, which was "very old" for a high-class sex slave, the buyer had wanted her. Then, the soldier had taken one last drag on his cigarette and tossed the butt beneath his combat boot. He looked at her lustfully, and told her that if his boss hadn't already sold her for a million dollars, he'd like to get a piece of her for himself.

Now, caged with her companions, Cara huddled with the two women, trying to calm them. She suddenly saw herself back in Tucson with her parents. How happy she'd been then! She and her sister Ali had grown up so loved, cared for, and supported. Family meant everything to her and yet, here she was, a thousand or more miles away, alone, helpless, and afraid.

In another week, the ship to Asia would take them all away, probably forever. *And then?* Cara simply couldn't fathom what would happen to her. The other three women did not even know their fate—just her—but Cara was sure they had been sold, too.

The door to the villa opened and shut. Cara's head snapped up, her eyes focused. There was the head soldier, and he was walking quickly toward their cell, his gaze was fixed firmly on her! She didn't know his name, but he terrified her. He was even crueler than his companions, clearly enjoying the pain he inflicted on the women. The soldier had a shaved head, stood six-feet, five-inches tall, with flat, gray eyes, and a four-day growth of beard. She knew he was Russian because she often heard him speak the language interspersed with Spanish, and sometimes, English slang.

Oh, no! Cara slowly stood up, her hands against her roiling stomach.

He opened the door with a jerk and stepped in. "You! Get over here!" he snarled in poor Spanish.

Cara froze. They were going to rape her! She saw the hardness in the man's eyes and noted his powerful muscles. He had an AK-47 hanging off a strap in front of him.

"Get over here!" he bellowed, and took a threatening step toward her.

Stunned, she forced herself to walk around the two women who were whimpering with fear, holding tightly to one another. Her heart was pounding so heavily she didn't know if she could make it to where he stood, his hands imperious on his hips, his glare eating into her like acid. Cara knew if she didn't obey instantly, he'd grab her by the hair and jerk her off her feet. They had never slapped her since she'd arrived. Was all that about to change now?

Lowering her eyes, head bowed, she walked to within six feet of the soldier. Earlier that day, three cars had driven up to the double wooden doors of the villa. The soldiers had opened the doors and allowed the visitors into the spacious area. Cara had seen one man leave each chauffeured car. All three were dressed in expensive business suits, and she could only guess what they were doing here. In the weeks since her capture, she'd sharpened her hearing, listening to snatches of conversation from the soldiers.

She'd found out that Emilio Azarola was a Sonoran drug lord who sent drugs across the border to the US and kidnapped young girls, some as young as age ten. They came from various cities, some from the United States, and others from cities and towns in Central and South America.

Azarola's sex-trafficking trade was growing, which was why this huge cell, that was roughly two-hundred square feet, had been built: it was a holding cell for his captives until their ships pulled into the dock at Puerto Nuevo. From there, children and young women would be shipped to the Middle East or Asia.

The soldier glared at her. "Come with me."

Shocked that he wasn't going to grab her or yank her by the hair, she hesitated, at a loss for words.

"Move!" he snarled, making a sharp gesture.

Cara leaped out of the cell and stood. Furtively, she looked around, trying to see if an escape was possible. Disheartened, she saw him looking at her, stripping her from head to toe with his colorless grey eyes. Now she knew what it felt like to be a mouse about to be pounced on by a tiger.

"Go to that door," he muttered, walking toward her, threatening her with his height and bulk. Instantly, Cara moved, but she suddenly felt weak, her knees turning mushy. *Oh, Dios . . . protect me . . . protect me . . .*

CARA JERKED AWAKE, breathing harshly, sweat running down her temples, her body damp, heart hammering. It took her a few moments to realize she was at home and no longer in that cell. She sat up, the sheet and blanket falling away from her cotton nightgown that clung damply to her body.

Dios, would the nightmares, the memories of her capture and weeks spent in that cell at Azarola's, ever end? She threw off the blankets. The room was still dark, except for a small nightlight, because full darkness scared her. Since her rescue, she continued to suffer from insomnia unless it was dark in her room, and her father had covered the window with a solid black cloth to help her sleep.

Remembering that it was late November, she sat on the edge of the bed. She tried to breathe more slowly, as Ram Torres had taught her. She was more than grateful that the ex-Navy SEAL was presently her security guard. Ali, her brave, brave sister, Ram, and his men, had rescued her and the German women from Azarola's fortress. In typical black-ops style, Ali and Ram had gone under the cover of night to get the captives out of their cell and away from that villa.

In a few days though, Ram was going back to Artemis, the security company he worked for. Ali was leaving three weeks after him because she had accepted a job at the same company. Cara pushed her disheveled hair away from her face, some of the strands clinging to her cheek. Looking at the clock, she saw it was nine a.m. The black cloth over the window hid the morning from her, and getting up, she padded on bare feet across the red tiles and pulled it aside. Her heart was still hammering. Every time she thought of her captivity, she could feel that rush of adrenaline shooting into her bloodstream. *Would it ever stop?*

Bright sunlight cascaded in, making her wince and hold her hand up to her eyes. Cara turned away and picked up her sandals, sliding them onto her feet. Her knee-length, brightly-colored, flower-print robe was draped over the back of a chair and she pulled it on, tying the sash around her waist. Pulling open the wooden door, she looked up and down the quiet hall. She listened, but couldn't pick up the voices of her parents, who would both be at work by this time.

Ram was usually out in the garage helping her father fix some items around the home. Her heart warmed as she thought of the tall security guard. He was the opposite of the Russian soldier, and over the past month, she no longer saw her captor's face, but Ram's instead. His presence gave her a sense of safety and peace. She relied on him to protect her from her wild imaginings about Azarola. She was terrified he would send his soldiers back to Tucson to kidnap her again. Ram, thank *Dios*, was the perfect guardian, and if anyone could help her heal from her capture, it was him. She was so grateful that he was there to keep her safe.

She wondered where Ali was. Her sister was the only person she could share her feelings with, although Ram often asked how she was doing.

She'd always say she was fine, but that was a lie. It was just too hard to open up to him right now—perhaps later.

She headed for the bathroom down the hall. To her left was the kitchen and living room area, and to the right, Ram's bedroom was opposite hers and Ali's was down the hall on the left. At the end of the hallway was the bathroom. She hurried towards it, desperate to wash off the fear sweat, that awful odor that made her wrinkle her nose. Her black hair swung around her shoulders as she walked, her sandals clip-clopping with each step against the red-orange tiles that lay throughout the house.

Cara had been born in the room that was now her bedroom. Her Yaqui-Indian mother hated hospitals and had refused to birth her two daughters anywhere but at home. Thinking of this made her feel good. When she focused on her parents or sister, she felt safer.

She pushed the door open to the huge bathroom, the alternating white and pale-blue tiles gleaming on the floor.

After a hot shower, scrubbing her flesh clean with her mother's herbal soap, she began to feel better. Another sage-scented soap made by one of the Yaqui women on the reservation, made her hair shine. Her mother was a strong woman, a leader, and she sat on the tribal council of the Pascua Yaqui south of Tucson.

Now, Cara truly appreciated being able to take a shower and wash her hair properly. These became huge events in her daily life since she returned home. The pleasure of running a comb through her wet hair afterward, of putting on a clean set of clothes, would never again be taken for granted. *Not ever.* She dried her hair, putting it into one long braid, and nudged it between her shoulder blades. She'd chosen a pair of tan cargo pants, a bright-pink tank top, and slipped on her leather sandals.

Her stomach growled. Since coming home, she had avoided breakfast, but today, for whatever reason, she was really hungry. Ali had been begging her to eat something for breakfast and right now, *huevos rancheros* in a warm, soft corn tortilla sounded really good to her. As a child growing up, it had been her favorite breakfast. Maybe, after five weeks of being home, she was finally starting to heal? Cara hoped so, because until she could find the courage to go outdoors, she couldn't walk to her school and teach kindergarten again.

As she padded to the kitchen, she spotted Ali shutting the garage door and coming inside.

"Hey," she called out, letting Ali know she was up and about.

Ali smiled brightly upon seeing her. "Hey yourself. How are you doing this morning?" she asked, walking into the kitchen.

"I'm hungry for the first time, Ali." She saw her sister's expression change from anxious to relieved. "Do you think I'm finally starting to heal?"

Ali hugged her tightly. "That sounds great! And yes, I think you're starting your healing journey. What do you want to eat?"

"*Huevos rancheros.*"

Laughing, Ali said, "Your favorite meal. Can I help you prepare it?"

"No, but sit down." Cara gestured to the large wooden table. "I love having your company." She spotted a half-full pot of coffee on the percolator. "Want coffee?"

"Of course," she deadpanned. "You can't have served in the military and not be a coffee hound."

Giggling, feeling much lighter than she had in a long time, Cara poured two cups and took one over to Ali. "Have you eaten?"

"Yes, Ram and I ate about 0700. I mean, seven a.m."

"I'm getting used to your twenty-four-hour clock," Cara said, going to the fridge and taking out two eggs.

Chuckling, Ali leaned back in the chair, the cup balanced on her thigh, watching her sister putter around in the kitchen. "We're going to be leaving for Artemis pretty soon. Our time with you is coming to an end," she murmured sadly.

"I'm really going to miss being here with you."

With a grimace, Cara said, "No more than me. And Ram? I'm going to miss him terribly. He really made me feel safe here." She cracked the eggs into a bowl, whisking them. "And so did you," she quickly added.

"Oh," Ali said with a grin, "Ram makes everyone feel like he can handle anything that comes up. It's just who he is. And I can see that his being here has really helped you. At least you can walk within the walled enclosure of our yard and our house now. And he's gotten you feeling safe about walking down to the end of the block and back. Those are huge steps, sis."

Cara nodded, taking bacon, shredded cheddar cheese, beans with green chilies, and other Mexican ingredients from the fridge. "I feel like such a coward compared to you, Ali. You're afraid of nothing."

Ali frowned, her voice turning low with emotion. "Listen, Cara, unlike you, I've never been captured and gone through what you have. I'm not sure I wouldn't be behaving just like you are. What you endured is . . . well . . . I don't even have words for it . . . it was terrible."

She placed the items on the counter and turned. "You've always understood me. I know Mama and Papa try, but you've gone to the heart of my wounding." She lightly touched her chest. "I know I'm not like you, Ali. You're bigger than life. You're fierce and you're a leader. I'm not like that. I'm quiet, I love teaching young children in kindergarten, I love gardening, and staying home. In many ways we're not alike, but you 'get' me. And I worry about how I'll handle it when you and Ram leave. I truly do."

Ali got up, leaving her coffee on the table, and came into the kitchen to help her sister put the meal together. "Look, the guy that's coming in to replace Ram? He was on the team that rescued you. Tyler Hutton. Do you remember him? He was our combat medic on that mission."

"That's so funny," Cara muttered, shaking her head. "When you came to rescue us, everything became a blur. Even now, I don't remember much about that night we escaped. Sometimes, though, I get dream fragments about it, or as I'm waking up, I'll have a vision of it."

"Because you were in shock and traumatized," Ali reminded her, choking up, and placing her hand on her sister's shoulder. "Tyler was there helping the German women, but he saw where you were being held. He's got a much better handle on what happened to you because he was part of your rescue team. That's a big plus!"

Cara shrugged and went back to preparing breakfast. "I know you're right. My feelings are so skewed. I don't trust anyone—especially men. Ram made it easy for me to trust him, but probably because you were here, too, Ali. You were the bridge I desperately needed between Mama, Papa, and Ram. And now, you're going to leave me." Glumly, she cracked the eggs into the hot iron skillet.

"You can Skype me any time you want, Cara. I'll be with you whenever you need to talk to me. Okay?" She placed two corn tortillas in another hot skillet, standing beside her sister.

"It's better than nothing. I just worry, Ali. I know you and Ram truly respect this Tyler guy, and you say he's great, but I feel scared again, like I did in that cell, surrounded by strange men."

"It's because you don't know what to expect." Ali quickly turned the tortillas, pulling over a plate to put them on. "After breakfast, let me show you some photos of him. He works at Artemis right alongside Ram."

"You've told me Artemis hires only the best." Cara placed the hot mixture into the two tortillas that Ali held on the plate.

"That's true. Tyler was a SEAL just like Ram. He was a Delta 18 combat medic. He's among the best trained in the world, and Ram worked with him on Wyatt Lockwood's SEAL team on and off for years. You're getting the best protection possible, sis." Ali turned off the gas stove and retrieved a napkin and flatware from the drawer.

"And you say he's gentle, thoughtful, and

listens well?"

"Yes, and he's sensitive, too," Ali said, straightening. "You'd never guess he was a SEAL. He doesn't have that hard layer of bravado they usually strut around with."

Cara brought the food to the kitchen table opposite the counter. "Would you like some, Ali? This is an awful lot. I can't eat it all. I think my eyes are bigger than my stomach." She managed a weak smile.

"Sure, be right back," and Ali skipped to the kitchen to find a plate and more flatware.

Cara gave her sister one of the tortillas filled with the spicy eggs, and Ali sat down opposite her at the table. "This smells so good!"

"Try it. If your stomach starts rolling around, stop eating," Ali advised, expertly rolling up her tortilla.

Cara did the same. "I'm so sick of my stomach rebelling in the morning. I used to eat a good, hearty breakfast before all this happened."

"Traumatic things happened after breakfast, though," Ali said softly, giving Cara a loving look. "I know. You told me, remember? Just do the best you can."

Cara took a tentative bite. She chewed slowly, afraid her stomach would act up. But it didn't. Maybe having Ali with her helped.

"Taste good?"

"Does it ever. I missed Mama's cooking so

much when I was locked up there."

Ali grinned, eating hungrily. "I know the feeling. I've been on way too many sniper missions for days or weeks at a time, and lived off meal replacement foods. Those MREs were so bland they were inedible until they finally put some hot sauce in them."

Cara nodded. She swallowed and waited, hating that her physical body's responses still reflected her abduction. She wanted to forget all of it, read books, watch movies with happy endings, and finally get to putter in her mother's huge garden. Gardening had always made her feel peaceful.

But now, the emotions she felt most often were terror and suspicion. Ali said it was the shock, and that slowly, these would be replaced with her normal emotions.

"You really trust this Tyler Hutton?" Cara asked quietly, holding her sister's golden gaze.

"With my life, Cara. That guy is a hundred-percent trustworthy. He will guard you with his life—and he'd give it in a split second without hesitation."

"I wish I could stop my brain from screaming that Azarola's coming back to recapture me and take me back to Sonora again."

Reaching out, Ali placed her hand over Cara's. "This is all part of the healing journey you're on, *pequeña,* my little one."

Cara felt her heart breaking as Ali spoke her endearing, loving nickname for her. She had grown up with it. Ali had always been her personal guard dog, protecting her from being bullied in school. She felt hot tears leap to her eyes. "I just want to forget all this, Ali. I want to get back to what I loved to do so much: teach kindergarten children. They're my whole life! I want that back." She closed her eyes, her voice trembling.

Ali gripped her hand. "It will come with time, Cara. I promise you that. Look how much you've changed since Ram and I stayed here with you. Tyler will continue that healing. He's a medic, after all. If anyone knows about regaining your health, it's him. Trust me on that."

Cara curved her fingers around Ali's hand, now bearing small scars and callouses on it. She hungrily absorbed the love that Ali was giving her right now. "I do trust you," she affirmed.

But could she trust this stranger coming into her life?

CHAPTER 2

November

TYLER HUTTON WASN'T very happy with himself. His palms were sweaty, something that only happened when he was *really* stressed out. He parked in front of the garage where his new personal security detail, Cara Montero, lived with her parents and eased out of the black SUV. He'd arrived at ten a.m. on a cool November morning. He had never been in Tucson, Arizona before, and liked the towering, pink adobe wall and the home it surrounded.

From a security perspective, he approved of the thick stucco wall and its five-foot height. The only weakness was the two-car garage. Did the family have some kind of internal and external security alarm service? Nowadays, anyone with the right software could open the garage and get into the house. It was one of the weakest, easiest access points for a burglar or those with darker objectives.

Tyler wiped his palms against his dark-brown chinos, chagrined by his nervousness. In the past, his PSDs had been males. He'd never had to guard a woman before, but Wyatt Lockwood, his boss at Artemis, had shrugged and told him he was fully capable of working with Cara. Especially because he was on the mission to help rescue her. Wyatt felt that connection would help stabilize the change in bodyguards for her.

"Just use your persuasive medical side with her and you two will get along fine," he drawled.

The dossier on Cara Montero was in his Toughbook laptop, tucked away in the briefcase sitting on the passenger-side seat. He'd gotten off a flight at the Tucson airport two hours earlier, changed his clothes, shaved, and hoped he'd look presentable to Cara. He'd combed his military-cut short black hair after pulling on a red t-shirt and a camel-colored sports coat over it. He was licensed to carry a concealed firearm and he wore one in a shoulder sling. The nylon holster rested against his lower ribcage out of sight beneath his sports coat.

Days earlier, the Artemis team had alerted the Tucson FBI office and local law enforcement officials that he was coming into their jurisdiction. He'd given them his license-to-carry permit number, plus a host of other items, including his photo, biometric iris recognition and fingerprints. As Wyatt had suggested, it was easier working *with* local law enforcement than keeping them ignorant of his presence. Especially if something happened that could prove messy, even dangerous.

He picked up his briefcase, but left his luggage in the vehicle, figuring he would take it out later. What concerned him was how beautiful Cara Montero looked in the picture he'd been shown. That may have been one reason he didn't want a female PSD mission—given his painful past. When Wyatt had handed him a color photo of Cara, he felt his whole world turn upside down. She looked so different from the starved, bedraggled woman he'd seen when they had rescued her in Sonora.

Of course, he couldn't admit that to Wyatt or he'd have yanked him off the mission. Tyler thought his overboard reaction may stem from his divorce from Lisa, his ex-wife, two years ago. Since then, he'd buried himself in one op after another, not coming up for air or even thinking about getting involved with another woman. That, along with his lingering PTSD, didn't make him a good candidate for another relationship anyway.

The guilt he still carried from damaging his marriage because of his PTSD symptoms never let up. He'd loved Lisa, but she finally admitted that she couldn't live with the "stranger," as she called him, who came home after too many SEAL deployments. She told him he wasn't the man she'd married and as hard as it was to admit it, Lisa had been right—and he told her so. They'd both cried together over what had happened to them, but in the end, they'd walked away from their marriage and wished each other the best. They were still friends.

Lisa had gone on to marry a civilian guy who adored her, and Tyler was more than happy for her. They still kept in touch occasionally, and Lisa's last email to him was that she was pregnant—something she'd always wanted.

Reading those lines, he felt as if someone had ripped his heart out. But when he'd stared down at Cara's photo, his heart swelled with such hope it damn near made him breathless. Tyler couldn't understand why he'd almost gasped upon seeing her because his heart was fine. He'd not had that reaction to her when they'd rescued her in Sonora.

Hell, maybe he was a lot lonelier than he realized. Was he subconsciously yearning for a woman in his life once more? He sure missed loving a woman, feeling that firm, soft skin and breathing in the scent of her hair. Listening to her laughter. Loving her feelings about herself and the world around her.

And now Cara brought all those thoughts

THE HIDDEN HEART | 27

and emotions roaring to the surface. She had the most compelling brown eyes—large, cinnamon hued, with a sheen of gold behind them—framed by thick, black lashes. He felt almost hypnotized by her eyes, never mind what the rest of her looked like. Ali had sent him several jpeg photos of her sister, and she was definitely the complete package. The fact that she was unmarried surprised him. Any man worth his salt would be interested in Cara just from a physical standpoint. For himself, though, he needed a woman who was his equal in smarts and gave him the same respect that he gave to her. He'd been raised in such a family, and unlike many of his SEAL friends in the Navy, he didn't see women as bedmates for one-night stands.

The front door opened and Ram Torres and Ali Montero greeted him with big smiles. The three of them had been close friends for many years. Ali waved, her eyes glistening with joy over his arrival. Both wore casual clothing, and no one would suspect that they were among the best black-ops warriors he'd ever known.

"Welcome home, Tyler," Ali called, striding ahead of Ram, her arms opening.

Tyler laughed as she threw her arms around his shoulders and squeezed the hell out of him. He gently embraced her and grinned back. "Good to see you, too, Ali. You're looking good. Happy, maybe?" He released her and she stepped aside as Ram approached, his hand held out toward Tyler.

"Yeah." She blushed and hooked a thumb across her shoulder toward Ram. "It's this guy's fault. He's made me happier than I've ever been."

Swallowing hard to push aside the sudden emotions, Tyler held her luminous looking eyes. He had known those emotions once, the breathless wonder of falling in love with Lisa. Now, Ali had fallen in love with Ram.

"Well," he rasped, his voice rough with emotion, "Congratulations. It couldn't happen to two more deserving people." He knew of their hard journey together. Somehow, they had moved from friction, to acceptance, to pure joy. Seeing the warm look Ram traded with Ali only made his smile deepen. Damn, he was happy for them!

"You look like a city boy," Ram teased, shaking his hand solidly.

"Is that an insult, Torres?"

Chuckling darkly, Ram released his hand. He and Ali stood on either side of him.

"You look right for the PSD," Ram admitted, losing his smile. He glanced over at Ali. "Want to give him a head's up?"

Tyler frowned. "What? Is Cara okay, Ali?"

"She's dreading meeting you, Tyler."

"Oh," he replied, his heart sinking.

"We've talked you up a lot, but she's still scared," Ram explained, keeping his voice low.

"Tyler," Ali added, "it's just where she's at right now. Ram has been like a pillar of protection to her since we all rescued her and those poor German women from Azarola's villa. She has good days and bad days."

"Or hours or minutes," Ram finished grimly.

"Sounds like she's still deep in trauma and shock over the kidnapping," Tyler said, understanding exactly what she was going through.

Nodding, Ali said, "Ram was damn good at what he did, and my little sister saw him in action during the rescue. Now that we're leaving, she's falling apart."

"That's understandable. I was busy helping the German women get to the helicopter while you and Ram got Cara out of there."

"Our whole team was responsible for getting those women freed," Ram pointed out. "You were a hero to those women."

"Yes, but you were the one who was at Cara's side when we made that run for the helo, Ram. I've seen shock keep a person down for weeks, months, sometimes years. It just depends on the person."

Ali reached out, patting Tyler's arm. "I think once she gets to know you, she'll settle down. Our biggest fear is that you two won't take to each other. Cara is overly sensitive about what other people think of her."

"Double jeopardy," Tyler agreed, grimacing.

"I didn't see anything in her file that said she was on any meds."

"Oh, no problem," Ali assured him, "Cara refuses all pharmacy-based medications. Right now, Mama gets her to drink a cup of chamomile tea when she's feeling anxious, but that's all she'll do."

"That's good," Tyler murmured. "Meds should be the last course considered. I read that your mother is a full-blooded Yaqui Indian."

"Yes. Mama knows a lot about herbs and other options that are less dangerous than things the doctors are trying to push Cara into taking. Things like anti-anxiety meds, sleeping pills—horrible stuff."

"Does chamomile help her, Ali?" Tyler asked.

"It does, for about an hour. Then the anxiety starts creeping back." She studied him for a moment. "Why? Do you have something up your sleeve, Tyler? A safe alternative to medication for Cara? Something natural?"

"I do," he said. "I've been working with a group of Army Delta 18 brothers and sisters about the anxiety and hyper-alert aspect of PTSD symptoms. There are some hopeful things out there that most vets, or victims like Cara, wouldn't know about yet. I intend, once she accepts me," he continued, crossing his fingers, "to talk to her about it and see if it appeals to her.

while he was in the SEALs. We all called him
'Doc Shrink'," he said, shooting Tyler a grin.

"Wow," Ali whispered, "I didn't know that!"
She went to stand near Ram, wrapping her arm
around his waist. "You sure don't look like a
shrink, Hutton."

"No one needs to know about that," he
mumbled, hating to be the center of attention.
He was here for Cara, not to spout the alphabet
about the degrees behind his name. "I try not to
let anyone know. Can you keep that from your
sister and parents? I know a lot of people have a
negative view of a psychiatrist or psychologist, as
if we're studying them like a bug under a micro-
scope. I'm sure at some point, I'll come clean
with her but for right now, let her know me as a
combat medic and bodyguard. I think that's
enough."

"Sure," Ali promised. "You have a nice, gentle way about you, Tyler. I really do think you're a
fit with Cara. Do you have any other questions
for us?"

"Not right now. Let's get this meeting over
with. I'm sure Cara is stressed over it and I want
to try to minimize her worries if I can."

"You're a medic," Ram said, gesturing him
ahead of them on the sidewalk. "No one has a
better bedside manner than you Delta dudes.
She'll fall in love with you, I'm sure."

Wincing inwardly, Tyler knew that Torres

was unmercifully teasing him, which was what SEALs did to each other. He said nothing, quickly taking the walk ahead of them and the two steps up to the red-tiled porch. The wood door had been sculpted by chisel, hammer, and love—by someone who was very talented with his hands. It was quite a work of art. There was a desert landscape with tall, handsome saguaro cactus and craggy buttes in the background that sometimes dotted the American Southwest. What he liked most was the mother deer and her fawn as the centerpiece on the door, the rising sun behind them. "What kind of wood is this?"

"That's Diego's work. He's Ali and Cara's father," Ram said, running his large hand across the smooth, polished wood. "It's mesquite and it took him two years to make this in his garage. The man is a true artist."

Ali snorted. "You're a terrific wood carver yourself, Torres." She looked over at Tyler, pride in her tone. "I'll show you the beautiful horse he carved for me. It's awesome."

"I'd like to see it," Tyler said, watching Ram open the door and gesture for Ali to go on in. They followed. As he stepped across the threshold, he took a deep, steadying breath. Now, he would finally get to meet the woman in the picture.

His heart filled with hope once again, despite his uncertainty about how Cara would feel toward him. Then, he remembered that she was in his care now. Tyler tried to steel himself inwardly. This was worse than being jumped by the Taliban hiding in an ambush!

Ali knocked lightly on Cara's bedroom door that was ajar.

"Come in . . ." Cara replied, softly.

"Hey, Tyler Hutton just arrived!" Ali said enthusiastically, stepping inside the room and leaning against the door.

Sitting on her bed, her knitting in her lap, she gave Ali an anxious look. "I heard you all come in. His voice sounded low."

"He's a medic, Cara. Our combat medics are some of the gentlest men and women we have. How are you doing?"

Grimacing, she placed her knitting aside on the bed. "Nervous. Anxious. Scared. The usual."

Ali came over and sat on the edge of the bed. "I know how hard this is for you. Ram has been your light in the darkness since we brought you home."

"No," Cara whispered, giving her sister a warm look as she reached out and curled her hand into Ali's. "*You* have always been the light in my life, and Mama and Papa, too. You're right though, Ram did give me an extra boost of feeling protected."

Squeezing her hand, Ali said, "Ram and I are as close as your computer screen. He's given you his Skype handle and you already have mine. If anything comes up, you can get on there and talk to us."

Cara bit down on her lower lip, her head dipping forward, her long curtain of black hair hiding her expression. "What's Tyler like? Is he nervous? Does he really want to do this? Or does he consider himself a babysitter? I remember being with him and the German women after you and Ram left to defend us half way to that meadow. Honestly, I was so out of it, I don't remember much at all as that team hustled toward escape."

Ali gave her a slight smile. "Why don't you ask him yourself? Tyler is an ex-SEAL. He can take anything you throw at him. Are you ready to say 'hello'? Ram's making coffee for all of us. We'll stay for a bit, but I really think the two of you need to just sit down and get to know one another, alone and uninterrupted."

"What if he's not a fit, Ali?" Cara detested the strain, the fear in her low voice as she searched her sister's calm face.

"Then he'll stay here until Wyatt can get someone else to take his place." She patted Cara's damp hand. "You have to create trust over time, with whomever is assigned to you. I'd give it one or two weeks and see how you get along with him."

"Is he like Ram? Will he give me space? Not

follow me around like a puppy?"

"I think that you need to communicate with Tyler about what sets you off and what makes you feel calm and protected. He's not a mind reader, Cara. He's really looking forward to hearing what you want; that's the best way he can serve you. You're not going to hurt this guy's feelings, believe me. SEALs are some of the toughest teasing dudes I've ever met. Tyler is quiet, he listens a lot and he asks good questions after you have your say."

Cara chewed on her lip some more. "Okay. *Dios*, I'm shaking!" She wrapped her arms around herself and looked away, shame filling her.

"Come on," Ali urged, tugging on Cara's upper arm. "He's not going to bite you."

Slowly rising, Cara looked at herself in a full-length mirror. She had thought long and hard about what to wear, finally settling on some cream-colored velour trousers, her comfortable white tennis shoes, and a light-gray top with three-quarter inch sleeves.

"I noticed you put some makeup on," Ali said.

"Just some lipstick and blush." She touched her cheeks. "I look so pale without it these days."

"Maybe Tyler will be able to coax you outdoors more? You used to be a tan coffee bean at this time of year."

"I did, didn't I?" There was lament in her

voice. "I'm not who I used to be, Ali." Grief stirred in her chest because Cara knew that was the truth.

"Well," Ali said, placing her hand on the door and opening it wider, "I think Tyler will find you very intelligent, sensitive, and kind. Just like him."

She frowned, hesitating at the door. "I'm so scared. I don't want to lose you and Ram. You've been my anchors since I got home."

Cara hated feeling like a coward. She had never been that way before her kidnapping. She straightened, pulling her shoulders back, and whispered, "Okay. Let's do this."

The hallway suddenly seemed so long to her as Ali walked at her side, one hand wrapped around hers. Cara needed her sister's touch right now. Ram and Ali had situated themselves so completely into her life, giving her the stability she needed after being threatened and examined as she stood naked in front of three men who inspected her like she was a breeding horse. Only Ram's quiet, unobtrusive presence, his ability to sit and listen to her, to ask such insightful and gentle questions into exactly how she was feeling, had helped her after returning home.

Cara wrestled with her anxiety and fear, wanting to appear normal. She knew deep down she would never be who she was again. When she stepped out into the living room, she saw Ram sitting in an overstuffed chair across from the couch where Tyler Hutton sat.

The moment he saw her, he quickly stood up—so did Ram. The medic was dressed casually, but it was his eyes—that sharp, eagle-like gaze, so blue and wide with intelligence—that captured her attention. He had broad shoulders beneath that tan sports coat and his red t-shirt brought out his deeply-tanned features, his oval face, and strong jaw and chin. He looked a lot different than when on that mission, his face covered with greasepaint, military clothing, and a weapon.

She liked his short black hair, thinking it was almost the color of hers. He had straight black brows above his eyes, his mouth beautifully shaped. Cara scanned him, seeking anything that would tell her he wasn't like those ruthless, hardened drug soldiers. She saw his eyes change, grow almost tender, as he held her unblinking stare. His mouth, the corners drawn in, relaxed, too.

And then, she knew. This stranger had kindness in him. How much, she didn't know yet, but the softening of his gaze as he regarded her, his mouth losing that tightness, soothed her. She moved her gaze to Ram, who was also studying her, but she was used to Ram's speculative looks at her. Ram smiled a little and winked. To Cara's surprise, it had an instant calming effect.

Ali led her to where her new bodyguard

stood. "Cara? This is Tyler Hutton, who I'm sure you remember, was on that mission to rescue you. Tyler, once again, meet my sister, Cara Montero."

Tyler slowly extended his hand toward her, allowing her to really look at his large, square hand. Hutton was easily six feet tall, maybe an inch or two shorter than Ram, but certainly athletic and powerful looking. She noticed small details now as never before. His hand was calloused across the palm and on the side of his index finger. There were all kinds of small white scars across his palm, and the back of his hand was dusted with a sprinkle of black hair.

She forced herself to offer her hand in return, feeling how cold her fingertips were. They got that way when she was in high-anxiety mode. Cara didn't know what to expect from this new man, but his hand was warm, dry, and gently engulfed hers. It almost felt like a feather lightly grazing her palm, not a true handshake.

"Hi, Cara. It's nice to meet you again under far better circumstances than before."

His voice was modulated, low, and she could hear the sincerity in his greeting. His eyes told her the same thing, and she saw care and concern for her in their depths.

Clearing her throat, tight with tension, she whispered unsteadily, "I-I'm a little off today. It's nice to meet you again, Tyler. I don't remember much about the rescue or you. I'm sorry. And to be honest, I'm feeling really shaky and unsure right now. It's me, not you." She felt him release her hand, but that warmth remained in his gaze and she clung to it, needing to feel his acceptance. And then, that deliciously sculpted male mouth of his drew slightly upward. It wasn't quite a smile, but it had tenderness in it that calmed her even more.

"I'm feeling the same, Cara. Nervous about meeting you. Hoping I meet your expectations . . . stuff like that . . . ."

Her heart thudded once and she melted beneath that partial smile. Something told her Tyler was probably one of the most honest men she'd ever met, but she wasn't about to cast that in stone—at least not yet.

"Why?" she asked, wanting to know. "Why would you be nervous about meeting me again?"

Tyler lifted his chin, looked at Ali and then at Ram, before moving his gaze back to hers. "I have really big shoes to fill with Ram here. And Ali's your sister. I have a lot to prove to you, and I hope I can meet your needs. Ram said you were good at communicating and I'd like to think I'm okay at it, too." He touched his heart with his hand. "My parents always taught me to speak from my heart, and I've found that the best way to reach out and touch others in a positive way."

"That's good to know," she offered, relief in

her tone, her confidence growing a little stronger. He was so tall, and his broad chest was hidden beneath that sports coat of his. She glanced at Ali. "There's no spare bedroom for Tyler. Where is he going to sleep?"

"Listen, Cara," Ram said, coming to her side, and grinning, "Tyler could probably tell you a ton of stories of us sleeping out on rocks, in caves, and freezing our butts off." He pointed to the couch behind where Tyler stood. "He gets the couch while I'm still here."

"And I'll feel very well taken care of," Tyler reassured Cara, smiling over at Ram. "He's right. We've slept and nearly frozen our butts off in some godforsaken places on this planet. This will be fine, believe me."

"Oh . . . good." She felt like a child, not the adult she used to be. Tyler didn't seem to think she was a child, however. "I'm sorry, but if I were my old self, before my kidnapping, I'd be racing to get pillows, sheets, and blankets out for you so it would seem more like a real bed."

"That's all right. Those things will come back to you in time," Tyler told her, again holding her skittering gaze. "Sometimes what we think we've lost has just been put on a back shelf in one our brain's many closets. I'm sure Ali and Ram will toss me a pillow and a few blankets when it's time to hit the sack tonight."

She clasped her hands, aware of how damp

and cold they felt even to her. Ali touched her arm.

"Ram and I are going to be in the garage after he gets us all coffee. If you need anything, come get us. If not, why don't you and Tyler sit down, enjoy the coffee, and get acquainted? Would you both like some?"

"I could sure use a cup," Tyler said, nodding his thanks. "What about you, Cara? Do you drink coffee?"

"Does the sun rise?" Ali teased, grinning at her sister.

"Yes, coffee, please. Thanks, Ali." Cara managed a slight smile over her sister's teasing and forced herself to meet Tyler's gaze once again. It was very hard for her to hold a strange man's gaze. She knew that to catch the attention of a drug soldier meant they would hassle her, put their hands on her in unwanted places, make her scream and fight back. No, it wasn't easy meeting a man's eyes anymore. She lifted her lashes and drowned in the warm blue gaze of Tyler Hutton. He wasn't her captor, but she still couldn't separate him from all the other men who had hurt and humiliated her.

"Where would you like to sit?" he asked.

Startled by the question, she considered it. Chewing on her lower lip, she looked at the chair where Ram had sat opposite the couch and coffee table. "There . . . I think . . ."

Why couldn't she just make a decision and sound sure of herself? She used to be able to do that. Forcing her feet in that direction, she went and sat down.

She was relieved that there was at least six feet between herself and her new bodyguard. Tyler turned and followed Ali and Ram into the kitchen. He helped her sister get the colorful mugs down from the cupboard and set them on a bamboo tray along with sugar, cream, spoons, and napkins.

Ram had been the same way with her, and that calmed Cara a bit. She knew Tyler was also an ex-SEAL, so they had the same background and training. Maybe that was what she was seeing?

Curious, she accepted the fact that with his tall, strong body and his broad shoulders thrown back with military pride, this was a terribly good-looking man! Cara hadn't known what to expect, but she *certainly* never expected Tyler to be someone who looked more like a model for the covers of the romance novels her mother read with such relish. When she'd first met him with greasepaint on his face, in her state of terror, she really didn't get to see the man.

If she trusted her intuition, she felt that Tyler was like a tiger that hid its claws. Like the big cat, when he walked she didn't hear his footsteps— Ram was the same way. That was why he always let her know from far away that he was coming to her. Ram never wanted to scare her or make her jump, and Tyler had that same walk. Were SEALs taught to walk in a certain way? Her curiosity was slowly overcoming her fears.

Cara sat back and relaxed a bit, resting her arm against the soft, colorful fabric of the chair's armrest, dotted with desert wild flowers. She heard Ram, Tyler, and Ali talking and joking with one another in the kitchen. It was obvious they were good friends, and her sister had told her a number of stories about her work with Ram and Tyler on operations. Tyler was with another SEAL team at J-bad that sometimes worked with her and Ram's team. She told Cara that they frequently joined up on missions together, which is why Ali thought so highly of Tyler.

Another trickle of calm quelled a bit more of her agitation. She knew that her big sister was a good judge of people. At one point, Tyler hugged Ali, and she hugged him, almost as if he were her brother and she, his sister.

Ali wasn't given to such spontaneity and that interested Cara even more. Maybe, just maybe, Tyler Hutton was who he seemed to be. In just a little bit, Cara would find out—one way or another . . .

CHAPTER 3

November

TYLER WATCHED CARA'S anxiety increase in her large, wide-set eyes as Ram and Ali left with coffee in hand for the garage, taking a little private time with each other. Her hand had trembled as she placed cream and sugar in her mug earlier when he set the tray down in front of her on the coffee table. He focused all his intuition on Cara. As a former SEAL, his sensing was heightened, almost psychic. How badly he wanted to wrap her into his embrace and just hold her, allow her to feel safe. There was a part of him, right or not, that felt a man should always protect women. He was hardwired for that and there was nothing he could do about it.

But to try to hold her was a fool's errand, he told himself sternly. The last thing Cara wanted was to be held by a man—men had hurt her.

However, he could broadcast quiet confidence to help Cara ratchet down her fears. Could they get along well enough for him to help her recover from her traumas?

"I don't know which of us is more anxious right now," Tyler admitted wryly. When he took off his coat, his shoulder harness and the pistol in it became visible. There was a flare of fear in her cinnamon eyes as she stared at the weapon, and he decided to take it off and cover it up with his coat that lay across the coffee table. The fear disappeared from Cara's gaze and he wondered if she was even aware of her reaction. "Ali and Ram are good friends of mine, Cara. We've worked with each other off and on throughout the years when I was a SEAL," he said, sitting down again. "We're kinda like brothers and a sister, but I think you already know that?"

She gave a jerky nod, her hands wrapped around the red mug resting in her lap. "Y-yes."

"Did Ali and Ram tell you a little bit about me?" He forced himself to pick up the coffee and appear at ease, taking a sip.

"They did. Ali showed me some photos she'd taken of you back in Afghanistan. She said you were with another team, but often, you went out together on missions."

"Yes, that's true. How did that make you feel?" he asked, trying to ignore her beauty, the way her black hair shined and fell in soft waves over her shoulders, the thick strands covering her breasts beneath the gray knit sweater she wore.

"Better. Right now, I'm skittish of any man, Tyler. I never used to be, but I can't stop my emotions from blowing up on me." She waved her hand in a helpless gesture. "My mind keeps telling me that every man is out to hurt me. I'm sorry, because you don't deserve that kind of reaction on my part. I wish . . . oh, *Dios*, I wish with all my heart I could stop that reaction and those thoughts, but I can't."

Nodding, he sipped more of his coffee, highly aware that his own body language was either going to relax her or spike her into an unconscious survival reaction. "I don't take it personally. In fact, I've worked with Afghan women who were raped or beaten by the Taliban." He watched the tension in her face reduce markedly.

"Ali said you were a wonderful healer, a combat medic who had saved many lives on the battlefield. Mama comes from a long line of medicine women in her tribe. When she heard Ali tell her that about you, she cried."

His brows rose. "Oh? Why would she cry?"

"Mama said that you were a medicine man in your own way. That you were a healer, too. She thought it was a good sign that Ram and Wyatt had chosen the right bodyguard for me."

"How did you feel when you heard that,

Cara?"

She managed a quirk of her lips. "Better. My family is centered on healing from nature and from our medicine people. Ali and I rarely went to a medical doctor's office. Mama always took us to a medicine woman on the reservation, first. We grew up with a very different way of getting healed. There were times when we did need to see an MD, but it was a rare thing."

"That's interesting. My mother, Dawn Hutton, is one-quarter Blackfoot through her mother's side of the family." Instantly, he saw Cara straighten, her full focus on him, excellent eye contact for the first time.

"Oh, that's so good to hear!"

Hearing the sudden wobble in her voice, he asked, "Why is that?"

"Because I'm sure your mother taught you some ways of her people? Her Blackfoot heritage?"

"No, she never mentioned I even had a relative who was Native American until I went through the top-secret clearance report from the US Navy. When I went home after graduating from SEAL training I asked her about it. She had only fuzzy memories about it, but it was better than nothing. I still think she has that gene, though. She loves nature, and from the time I could remember, I was always going out into the mountains around Philipsburg, Montana, where I was born. My father is a gem miner, a hunter, and fisherman. Mom hikes to this day. She's very much an outdoors person."

"That's a wonderful way to grow up in the wilds of the mountains."

"It was. Mom used to call me her 'wild child.' I always liked going home and visiting my folks when I came in from a deployment. My dad and I would go trout fishing, which I always looked forward to, and as a kid I hated wearing shoes. I'd go barefoot unless it was winter. I didn't like the loss of freedom. I preferred the contact I had with the earth through my feet."

Cara's face reflected a bit more calmness. Maybe this was the way to introduce himself to her: to remain vulnerable and let her get to know him personally, not just as a bodyguard. All those dry rules and information he had to share with her could wait for another time.

"Ali and I were the same way! That's an amazing coincidence, because we all hated wearing shoes—and we all have Native American blood in us!"

He smiled a little, setting the mug on the coffee table. "I know you're a kindergarten teacher. Do you have any rug rats who hate shoes or don't want to wear them when they're in your class?"

"Rug rats? What's that?" she asked, tilting her head.

"Sorry, it's a military term for children. A nice one. It's not an insult."

"Oh." She frowned. "It doesn't sound very nice."

"I agree, but military parents love their children just as much as civilian ones do. I've only been out of the Navy for two years, and where I work, at Artemis, it's full of ex-military people. My military lingo is still strong in me but I'll try to translate that into civilian language for you."

"You don't have to do that. When Ali comes home, she starts talking in an alphabet soup of weird acronyms and oddball words." She managed a hesitant half smile. "My parents and I get a lot of laughs out of some of them."

"It's a kind of shorthand," he agreed. Little by little, Cara was relaxing. She was now leaning against the pillow on the chair. As a SEAL, he had been taught to recognize subtle variations in body language because it could save his life in certain circumstances—and it had.

Seventy percent of human communication was non-verbal and through the body—gestures, tonal inflection when they spoke, and facial expressions—not the spoken word. When Cara first sat down in the chair, she had crossed her ankles beneath the coffee table. Now, her one leg was across her knee in a much more relaxed pose than before. Locked up legs or arms meant she was feeling threatened—which was the last thing

Tyler wanted as a response to him.

On the other hand, he tried to ignore her in certain ways. She was gorgeous in person, and the living room's skylights cast hues of gold on her skin. The light sifted through her eyes and dappled on the strands of her hair. On top of that, her every gesture was ultra-feminine and graceful.

"Speaking of language, Ali thinks it's funny," Cara added, "when Mama, Papa, and I sit there at the kitchen table during dinner, and we're talking about something, and then Ali will take off in her own language."

"We call it 'mil-speak'," Tyler offered. "And if I drop into it, stop me and I'll rephrase, okay?" Cara nodded and perked up. No one liked being spoken to in a language they didn't understand. It created barriers, not doors that could be opened between the two parties.

"Like medical doctors talking to us in 'medi-calese'," Cara said, wrinkling her nose with distaste. "I don't like the drugs that doctors use on us. Never did. I know they can be useful at times, but we were raised on herbs, ceremonies by our medicine people, and natural remedies."

Tyler was a paramedic and wondered if she would hold that against him. Wisely, he decided not to go there. "Engineers have their own mysterious language, too." He smiled a little. "I like people who are honest and forthright, and I think you're built that way, too."

She grew serious, studying him. "I don't know how else to be but honest, Tyler. Ali says what you see is what you get with me. I love children because they are completely honest, too. Maybe that's why I love teaching so much: what you see is what you get with each child."

"I'll always be up front with you, Tyler. Ali said she's worked with you, and that she felt you were the right person to replace Ram."

"I know you don't trust me yet and that I have to earn that right from you, Cara. But I know you trust Ali's experience and insights. She and I worked together off and on for years when we were still in the military. In our business of black ops, we can die in a second. The people we worked with always had our back and we had theirs. Ali saved my life more than once, and so did Ram. What we share is far more than just friendship. We're sort of like a cosmic family."

"She told me a little about that. I mean, she doesn't tell us about top-secret aspects of her job, but she gave me a peek into who you were out in the field. I think she wanted me to know that in combat, you were someone she or Ram would turn to for support and help."

"Yes, that's right. That's what it means to have the other person's back." He hesitated for a moment, his voice going low with feeling. "Cara? I have your back. We need to work as a team to keep you feeling safe."

She looked away for a moment, her lips compressing. Finally, she met his gaze. "I'm just not myself, Tyler. I thought I knew who I was until I got kidnapped. Those three weeks of hell on earth changed me so much, there are hours or days when I don't recognize this new self."

"You nearly died," he said gently. "I read the report that Ram wrote up, and I was given the report from the CIA who debriefed you at the Davis-Monthan Air Force Base after you were rescued." He saw her cheeks blaze pink, realizing how ashamed she was that he knew everything that had happened to her.

"You know, because of my own injuries, my PTSD, I understand exactly what you're saying. I returned home and my parents didn't recognize me, either." He saw her face fill with sympathy, her lips parting. "I'm telling you this for a reason. I remember I was the same way as you are right now. It took me time to work through all the things that had happened to me and come out on the other side of it. I'm more like my old self nowadays, but in some ways I'll never be exactly the same person I was before I joined the SEALs."

She placed her hand against her throat, staring at him, the silence thickening. "Were you up and down emotionally? Happy one moment and sad the next? Did you suddenly start crying without any reason?"

"Yes, all those things happened to me—and a lot more. I had pretty ugly flashbacks and nightmares." And it was those last two that had destroyed his marriage.

"I-I just don't feel normal, Tyler. Sometimes I want to crawl out of my skin and hide. I feel so much grief sometimes that I can barely breathe. And the anxiety—it's always there, always lurking around like some kind of uncaged monster prowling around inside me. And I have absolutely no control over it."

"I've gone through all of those phases, too," he assured her. The tears sparkled in her eyes and he sensed she was very close to crying. He pulled out a white linen handkerchief from his back pocket and stretched his hand outward. "Take this. I got a lot more in my suitcase."

"Thank you. I'm so ashamed for crying so much," she said, her voice barely a tearful squeak, as she pressed his white handkerchief against each eye.

"Don't be," he urged. "I've lost count how many buckets of tears I went through. It's better to let it out than sit on it, Cara. I've seen too many people fight it, and they ended up killing themselves months or years later. It's not worth it." He knew of her depression, knew that at one time, Ali had emailed him and told him that Cara had talked about dying because it was simply too painful to go on that way.

She gripped the handkerchief between her fingers, looking down at it. "I was afraid that you would think I was crazy. My poor parents have never seen me act like this. If Ram and Ali hadn't been here through the worst of my ups and downs, I'm not sure my parents could have handled it as well as they have. They've suffered so much for me. They want me well . . ."

"It won't always be like this, Cara. You're less than six weeks into your recovery. Most people I know aren't as far along as you are, you need to know that. Keep your hope up, okay? If you think it's a good idea, I can share some stories of my own walk with PTSD with your parents. I can tell them that you're much further along in your healing process at this stage than many others. I think hearing it from someone else who has walked the same trail will be helpful. Do you?"

She sniffed and then blew her nose. "Yes, I think they need that. Ram was really good at explaining what was going on with me. They love Ram. And we're all hoping he and Ali will get married someday. They're so right for one another."

Tyler grinned. "Yes, they're a good fit for each other." He saw Cara fighting to lift her head and meet his gaze. So many abused children and women feared looking into a man's eyes. To meet his gaze meant so much to him because it was her first step toward trusting him.

"Do you have any questions for me, Cara? Do you want to tell me the boundaries that make you feel safe? What you expect from me? We can go over what I need from you later." He watched her expression remain calm, another sign that he'd passed the first step in their exploratory session with each other.

"I do, but right now I'm so exhausted that I need to go lie down. Stressful meetings tire me out terribly. And I have twenty-five sweaters I've knitted as a Christmas present for my kindergarten children that I have to gift wrap."

"Maybe I can help with wrapping them when you're ready? I'm pretty good at it."

"That would be wonderful," she said, giving him a hopeful look. "I wasn't sure what you were allowed to do as my bodyguard." She warmed as she saw him smile, his blue eyes glinting.

"I need to be in your general vicinity, Cara, and I'm more than happy to help where and when I can. Wrapping gifts sounds like a lot of fun."

"Ram and Ali went out and bought the paper, ribbons, and tags last week."

"I'll wrap if you'll do bows, okay? I'm not very creative," he offered, holding up his two big hands.

She managed a slight smile. "We'll get along fine, then."

"I'm going to go get my luggage from my vehicle and settle in. I'm sure Ali and Ram will take me around and acquaint me with the house and the outdoor area while you nap."

"Good . . ." She blotted her eyes one more time. "If I were in your shoes, I wouldn't be looking forward to caring for a person like me."

He managed a wry smile. "I've found that we all need help and support from time to time. Right now, it's your turn. Nothing to be ashamed about."

"I'm not a strong leader like Ali, but I was so confident, super positive, and idealistic. I could look people in the eye, too. I loved life, I loved living it, and my dream of being a teacher meant everything to me."

"Then," he said, slowly standing up, "you'll get those pieces of yourself back again, Cara." She looked skeptical.

"Is the *real* you back, Tyler? The person your parents knew?"

He picked up the emptied mug and placed it in the tray. "For the most part, yes. My storm of emotions took over my life for a while, but with the right help, I'm pretty much back to who I was before it happened. It took me a couple of years." He took her empty mug and placed it next to his, picking up the tray. "You have that to look forward to. Go get your sleep. I'll either be outside or somewhere in the house." He didn't want her to have to look for him under the present circumstances. Even going outside was a big deal for her right now and he didn't want to stress her even more. "I'll see you after you wake up," he said.

"Yes, see you then . . ."

HOW THE HELL was he going to shut off his libido? It hadn't been this active since the divorce! There wasn't anything about Cara that he didn't absorb like a thirsty sponge. She was attractive, intelligent, and built like a gazelle. Ali was taller than her sister and medium-boned, not slender like Cara. As he rinsed the cups in the kitchen sink and placed them in the dishwasher, he kept one ear cocked in Cara's general direction. He heard the soft swish of her footfalls coming his way from the living room and glanced up as she headed down the hallway where her bedroom was located. She was walking with her arms around herself, a sure sign of feeling unsafe.

Well, damn.

On the plus side, he felt as if he'd made a good initial connection to Cara. Reminding himself that she had unexpected cortisol hormone surges brought on by her condition, she could be having one right now that had nothing to do with the fragile link he felt they'd established. Tearing his gaze away from her, he finished up his kitchen duties and headed off to the garage to talk with his friends.

Opening the door, he saw Ram on a stool, carving what looked like a raptor, and Ali was on a stool opposite, watching him. They both lifted their heads in unison as the door opened, swiveling their attention toward him.

"Well?" Ali asked, pulling over a third stool for him to sit on. "How did it go with Cara?" She looked at her watch. "Thirty minutes is good, Tyler. Normally, she finds talking tiring and throws in the towel about ten or fifteen minutes into it. Since I've been home with her this is the longest she's chatted with anyone, including our parents." She grinned, holding out her hand toward him after he sat down. "Major congrats. You must have magic with her."

"Yeah," Ram said, wiping his hands off with a nearby towel. "We never talked that long. Must be your bedside manner coming online, Hutton."

Rubbing his palms slowly down his slacks, Tyler said, "I'm not sure."

"Can you tell us what you talked about?" Ali pleaded.

"Sure." He launched into a brief review of the topics they'd discussed. Afterward, he saw hope shining brightly in Ali's golden eyes.

"I didn't know you had Native American blood in you!" she gasped.

THE HIDDEN HEART | 63

He gave Ali a wry look. "I never thought it was important."

"Well, it sure is to us! Mama's tribe originally came from northern Mexico. Many of them left because Mexican soldiers were killing the tribe and forcing them to move out of their ancestral lands. The Pascua Yaqui came to what was later known as southern Arizona. They have a huge reservation south of Tucson."

"It seemed like her Native American background was very important to Cara," he agreed.

"Half her kindergarten class is comprised of Yaqui children and the other half is Hispanic," Ali said. "She knows the language of our people and is a fluent speaker. She also speaks Spanish. She's teaching her kids to speak English well so they can go to college, get good paying jobs, and have a life here that fulfills the American dream."

"That's commendable," Tyler agreed. "In my family the Native American lineage was sort of a skeleton in the closet. I didn't even know about it until it was uncovered in the FBI investigation to award me top-secret clearance. It was from my great-great grandmother, on my mother's side of the family."

"A lot of people in the US hid that information until around 1990 because they were ashamed of it," Ali agreed sadly. "But Mama celebrates our lineage. She's one of the stewards of our nation. Did you know that?"

"No. I have a lot to catch up on, don't I?"

"Mary will take care of that," Ram assured him, chuckling. "She's proud of her blood and tribe. I think Ali got her mother's fierce warrior genes and Cara got Diego's artistic genes. You'll like their father a lot. He's soft-spoken, gentle, and kind—just like Cara. He dotes on his daughters and worked his ass off ten to twelve hours a day to give them the education they received. And," Ram gestured to the carving tools near his hand, "he's an incredible artist and furniture maker. I'm going to miss being here because we had this man cave of ours where he showed me some tricks of the trade for making good furniture pieces."

Holding up his hands, Tyler said, "I'm no good at those things. I can fix a car, though."

Ali laughed and patted his shoulder. "My father will adore you. He's pretty mechanical himself, and will always welcome someone like you to help around the house."

"That's what I did," Ram told him. "I looked for things that needed to be fixed, painted, cleaned, or picked up. The girls' parents both work hard five days a week. Cara moved back in with them full time after college and until her kidnapping, she did a lot of cooking at night for them, performed major housework, weeded Mary's garden, and helped them with bills."

"I see. Has she always been close to her parents?"

"Yes," Ali said. "I had the wanderlust, the need for risk-taking and excitement. Cara is just the opposite. When we were little girls, I wanted to be some kind of heroine who saved people's lives and she wanted to settle down, be a kindergarten teacher, have a brood of kids of her own, and be happy with our parents nearby."

"Too bad childhood dreams don't always come true," Tyler murmured.

"Don't go there," Ram growled. "You're right. But having been around Cara for over a month, I've found her to be one of those people who is perfectly happy with getting married, having kids, and being a teacher. That's all she wants out of life."

"Unlike us," Tyler said, giving Ram a black-humor kind of look.

"Yeah, unlike us, for sure. But we need people like Cara because they become anchors for tumbleweeds like us. We become tethered to them and orbit around them."

Wincing inwardly, Tyler thought of his ex-wife, Lisa and how much she had been an anchor to his life until it spun out of control. "We all need an anchor," he agreed heavily.

"Ram will leave shortly and I'll remain here for two or three weeks until I'm sure leaving won't upset Cara," Ali told him, changing the subject. "We're trying to make this an easy transition for Cara, although I know she's counting the days and doesn't want Ram to leave at all."

"Right now," Tyler said, pushing his fingers through his short hair, "she's like a child who has just had her safety net torn away from her."

"She's come a long way in a short amount of time," Ram said, pride in his tone. "Cara's just as strong as Ali, but in a different way. She's digging deep and making, what we think, is good progress."

"I'm hoping to win more of her trust, and I'll try a little pivoting to smooth over the fact that you two are leaving soon. At least she has her parents here and I think that's valuable."

"It is," Ali assured him. She gave Tyler a worried look. "I don't know what you have up your sleeve, but Cara needs to be distracted."

"How often does she go out on the back porch and swing?" he asked.

Ram rubbed his jaw. "Maybe three or four times a week. Why?"

"Movement lulls humans into a calm. A rocking chair will do it, a cradle swinging a little, or a porch swing moving back and forth, has the same effect on our parasympathetic nervous system. It's a little thing, but an important one. I'm going to try to maneuver her in that direction."

"Yes," Ali whispered, "I think that's a great

idea. She does love to sit out on the porch swing and knit. Next to weeding Mama's garden, that's her second favorite activity."

"Cara mentioned she had just knitted a sweater for each of her kids at school. That's a lot of knitting, isn't it?"

"She does this every year because the kids are growing like little weeds and she wants them warm for the winter. Most of the children come from very poor families. Maria, her teaching substitute, gave her each child's size. The sweaters are all done and Cara wants to start wrapping up the presents tomorrow. I told her we'd all help."

Brightening, Tyler said, "We just discussed that and I told her I'd be happy to help, too."

"How did she react?" Ali wondered.

"Positively. She said she was good at ribbons and I volunteered to do the wrapping."

"Then," Ali said coyly, "I think that kind of activity is a trust-building opportunity for both of you. Ram and I will take off for a few hours to give you more time with one another. It may help Cara settle in with you."

"I agree. Has she wanted to go back and start teaching?"

"Not yet," Ali warned. "She's afraid of that two-block walk. That's where she got kidnapped, about a block away from the school when she was going home after class in the late afternoon."

Tyler felt hopeful. "The good news is that she's still connected with her kids, Ali. That could prove to be just the push she needs to make herself go back to school. I realize she isn't ready to teach just yet, but I'll bet the kids love and miss her, right?"

"Oh, indeed they do. They worship Cara. She's like a second mother to them. Do you really think the pull to get back to her kids might help her break this self-imposed prison she's put herself in? Even my parents, when I talk with them, say Cara is resisting a return to her regular life. I agree with them. But I didn't go through what she did. I might feel the same way. I just don't know. Do you?"

"It's a double-edged sword," Tyler said. "If she's not pushed out of the parental nest, at a certain point in her recovery she might regress."

"Meaning?" Ram asked.

"Meaning she might settle for remaining at her parents' home and avoid a return to teaching." He gestured toward the door that led to the kitchen, "She might choose to settle for less because the world has become too frightening and overwhelming. But in my book, that's not living."

Ali cursed softly. "You're right. That's not good, Tyler. I wish you'd known Cara before the kidnapping. She was so idealistic and caring, loved being a kindergarten teacher. She was just in love with life."

"What about a boyfriend?"

"Ugh," Ali muttered. "Yeah, she had a couple of them over the years. All dirt bags in my opinion. Cara's idealism attracted the wrong kinds of guys into her life, if you ask me. Not that I was around a lot to get to know them."

"What about the last one? Did she have a relationship before her kidnapping? That's the one I'm interested in," Tyler said. He really didn't want her to have a relationship, which was very selfish on his part, but Cara was far too lovely not to draw the eye of every man who saw her.

Ali slid off the stool, crossing her arms as she slowly walked around the garage, frowning and in thought. Finally, she stopped, turned, and looked over at him. "I met Colin Stein twice, Tyler. When I came home from deployments down in Mexico while working for the CIA, I met him. He's twenty-six, Cara's age. A jerk, if you ask me."

"In what way?"

"He's a civilian," she began, "a creep, someone who's jealous, mouthy, and immature. He treated Cara like a slave. Finally, I stepped in. Then, he tried to manipulate the situation and make it look like I was the one at fault. He kept repeating the same thing three times in a row, that stuff was my fault, that I was reading things the wrong way. Like he's going to convince me if he keeps saying it?" She snorted and glared over at Tyler. "If that blond douche bag comes crawling back into her life, just shoot him."

Ram laughed. "Come on! You don't really mean that, Ali."

"I guess not," she fumed. Giving Tyler a hard look, she said, "Cara sees only the good in people, she's not a realist. She doesn't see a wolf in sheep's clothing like Colin."

"Did he show up after she was kidnapped?"

"He called over here and my mother answered the phone. She told him she'd been kidnapped."

"And?"

"He just hung up."

"What about since she's returned home?"

Shaking her head, she said, "No one's heard from him, but don't put anything past him. He gives me a really bad vibe, Tyler. But for whatever reason, Cara doesn't pick up on it. It drives me crazy. I can see an idiot like him coming from a mile away. Why can't she?"

"Maybe she sees the goodness in him, instead, and not his manipulative side?"

Ram managed a sour grin. "I never met him, so I can't help you out here, Tyler."

"My take on Colin was that he was chasing Cara down to get her into his bed and that's the brutal truth."

"Okay. But given his personality, Ali, if he

does come here to see her, what should I do?"

"Beat the shit out of the little turd."

Bursting out into guffaws, Ram laughed just as hard as Tyler did. "Ali!" the men said in unison.

"You asked," she snapped, her hands on her hips, glaring at both of them. "He's not honest or up front with her, Tyler. Cara is my baby sister." She poked her chest with her thumb. "It's my responsibility to keep guys like Colin out of her life."

"So," Tyler teased, "if he comes to the house door and I answer it, I'm supposed to drop kick him off the front porch. Right?"

"Damn straight," Ali spat. "Because I'll make sure he *never* gets close to Cara again." She went over and poked Tyler in the chest with her index finger. "And your job is to protect Cara from him!"

"Don't worry," soothed Tyler. "I'll make it happen. But what if she *wants* to see him at some phase of her recovery?" Given Ali's readout on Colin, he really wanted to keep him away from Cara.

Ali stared hard at Tyler. "If I find out you let Colin see her again I'll fly back from Virginia and shoot you myself. Does *that* answer your question?"

CHAPTER 4

November

CARA AWOKE SLOWLY, hearing laughter floating down the hall toward her closed bedroom door. Earlier, she'd begged off to go take a nap and Tyler had given her a nod and an understanding look. She sat up, pushing her hair away from her face, looking at the clock hanging on the lavender colored wall opposite her bed. It was three p.m. She'd slept more than two hours. Tired of being tired, she sat there wondering when she'd get her mojo back. When would her vitality and desire to leave this house return?

Her thoughts turned to Tyler Hutton and peace descended upon her, dissolving the heaviness that hung about her as she closed her eyes, picturing his face. His shy, boyish smile had captured her heart, and even when he remained serious and intensely focused, she thought of that first smile—the one that had made her trust him without question.

Feeling better, even a bit more energetic, she opened her eyes again, stood up, smoothed down the fabric of her trousers, and walked down the hall to the bathroom. Usually, she avoided looking into the mirror because what she saw scared her—the haunted look in her large brown eyes was more like an imprisoned animal than a human being. But this time for some reason, she went in, combed her hair, and regarded her pale face. For the first time since returning home, she actually cared about what she looked like. Opening a drawer, she pulled out a pink lipstick, added just a tad of blush to her pale cheeks, and immediately felt . . . prettier. Maybe it was a sign she was getting better?

Cara looked for symbolic small handholds, as if climbing a steep, unending vertical cliff within herself, each upward movement toward the top meant she was healing. Even if it was just a baby step forward, it was progress.

More laughter drifted past the door and she opened it, standing there, listening to Ram, Ali, and Tyler sharing stories in the kitchen, followed by more laughter. It made her smile. She loved Ram like a brother. He'd done so much for her. He was a true hero in her eyes, like her brave sister had always been. Straightening and squaring her shoulders, she decided she wanted to join them, wanted to feel like a part of something positive. Cara was so tired of crying, so tired of feeling weak and helpless. That just wasn't her!

All heads swiveled her direction as she walked into the kitchen. Her heart thumped as Tyler gave her a warm, welcoming smile, pushing away from the kitchen counter, and walking toward her. She felt his protectiveness in his casual, relaxed movements, knowing that beneath that sports coat he carried a weapon.

"Hey," she called to all of them, "what's so funny? Can I laugh, too?"

"Oh," Ali muttered, "did we wake you up, Cara?"

She managed a small smile. "No, I was already coming awake. You three sounded like you were having so much fun out here I wanted to be a part of it." The softened look she saw in Tyler's eyes fed her hope that she would get better. She looked up at him as he halted. "I'm okay," she said, sensing his concern.

"I can see that. We were just making a pot of coffee and were going to sit down at the kitchen table. Come on over and join us?" He reached out, cupping her elbow, not possessively, but more to guide her toward where Ali and Ram were standing in the kitchen.

"I'd love to," she said. Cara was always self-aware and used her intuition with her children. Now, she was using it to sense Tyler, who walked at her side. He wasn't crowding her or trying to force her to do anything she didn't want to do—unlike Colin. Frowning, she could see the difference between her missing-in-action boyfriend and this man. Tyler didn't walk too close to her, but not too far away, either.

"Is this what a bodyguard does?" she asked him. He cocked his head in her direction, that same boyish smile appearing.

"Somewhat. Am I making you uncomfortable?"

She shook her head. "No, you aren't." But she wasn't about to tell him how good, how protected, his closeness made her feel, either. Besides, she couldn't explain all these magical, mystical sensations and feelings she received from another person. Ali understood it. Her mother, Mary, had the same thing, only she called it "being intuitive." Ali said it was more than that, it was psychic ability to monitor others, situations, and her surroundings.

Cara wanted to tell Tyler about this family ability, but was afraid he wouldn't believe her. He'd certify her as *loco*.

When they reached the L-shaped counter area, Tyler dropped his hand away from her elbow and she rested her hips against the counter next to her sister. Ram had just plugged in the coffeemaker. Tyler went to a nearby cupboard and retrieved four bright-blue mugs and brought them to the table. Ram brought over the cream from the fridge and sugar from the counter.

Cara looked over at Ali. "I could get used to this." She saw her sister's golden eyes gleam, that wolf-like grin stealing across her lips.

"SEALs are used to working as a team, Cara. They don't stop to think if it's a woman serving them coffee or not. They see the four of us as a team and whatever needs to be done by the team is done without thinking about it."

"Nice," Cara whispered.

"You look better."

"Yes. I got some sleep. Made up for what I lost last night."

Nodding, Ali said, "You look well . . . maybe happier."

That was Tyler's influence, but Cara said nothing. "Yes. Let's go sit down."

"Yeah," Ali walked with her to the table. The guys finished setting the table, adding paper napkins and spoons, then sat down with the two women. Tyler sat opposite Cara and Ram grabbed a plate of cookies that Mary had baked last night: peanut butter, Ram's favorite! Mary had made them especially for him because she knew his penchant for peanut butter anything. He'd found out from Ali earlier that she'd put the bug into her mother's ear and Mary had gone out of her way to make these cookies for him. Ali sat at the head of the table with Cara at her right.

"Cookies," Ram announced proudly.

Chuckling, Tyler said, "Watch it, ladies. He's got them counted and he's going to make sure he gets his share. Better grab yours quick or there won't be any left."

Cara laughed, enjoying the familial-like teasing. She saw Ram's cheeks pink up and knew he was caught red-handed by Tyler. Ali had warned her that SEALs were constantly gigging one another like this. As Ram placed the plate between them, Cara picked up one and set it on her napkin.

"Are you three always like this?" she wondered, giving Ram a warm look as he straightened.

"Pretty much," he said.

"How many cookies do I get?" Cara teased him.

"You can have as many as you want," Tyler said, meaning it.

"Yes," Ali chimed in, "you're underweight and we want you to get some more meat on your bones."

"Take her at her word," Ram warned with a chuckle, placing two more cookies on Cara's napkin.

"Oh, I can't eat that many!" she exclaimed, holding up both her hands.

Tyler moved his chair back and walked over with the coffee pot. "Save 'em for later," he suggested, pouring into her mug first, then Ali's.

Ali giggled and gave Cara a comic look. "Tyler's right. Ownership is nine points of the law."

"Hey!" Ram called from the counter, "make sure I get at least a few. Mary made those for *me*."

Tyler set the half-empty pot on a metal trivet in the middle of the wooden table and sat down next to Cara. "You know what they say about the early bird getting the worm, right, Torres?" He reached for a handful of cookies.

Groaning, Ram hurried back to the table, sat down, and saw there were exactly three cookies left on the plate. He gave them all a look of disbelief. "Oh, come on! Those are my fave cookies! Mary made 'em for me! Couldn't you have left me more than three?"

"Hey, Torres," Tyler deadpanned, his hand over his stash next to his mug, "There were a dozen there. The four of us get three cookies each. You weren't cheated."

Snorting, Ram gave Tyler a dark look. "Good thing the women are here."

"Yeah, I know. We'd be fighting over those cookies if they weren't!" Tyler laughed heartily, biting into the first one.

Joy threaded through Cara. It was the first time since coming home that she'd actually laughed. Touching her heart, she wanted to absorb this feeling like the first faint ray of sunlight finally piercing her inner darkness.

Ali slid her a merry look. "Guard your cookies, Cara." She hoisted a thumb in Ram's direction. "You don't know it yet, but he's the original cookie monster."

Tyler snickered, his hand over his other two cookies because Ram was within striking distance of them. "That's true. Ali, I remember one time when our team was working with yours in an Afghan village. Your mom had baked you some cookies, wrapped each one in foil, and put them into a three-pound coffee tin so they wouldn't be crumbs by the time you got them."

"Ohhhhh, that incident." Ali rolled her eyes, giving Ram a hilarious look. "Yeah, Ram got wind of them, Cara. We had two people assigned to every hut within the village. I had hidden my coffee tin of cookies in my pack, in my hut. When I went in there to grab an MRE for lunch, I found Ram hanging around outside the hut. I asked him what was going on because at that time, we were not friends—and he wasn't my roommate, so I got suspicious right away."

"Why?" Cara wondered, seeing the guilty look coming to Ram's features.

"Because he was going to go in there, riffle through my pack, find my cookies, and steal some." She looked at Ram. "Weren't you?"

"Guilty," Ram admitted heavily. "You caught me in the act."

Tyler snickered. "At least you're honest

about your thievery, Torres. That says something good about you."

"But I hadn't done it yet," Ram defended.

Everyone burst into laughter, including Cara. She didn't know what magic was happening, but she was sure it was because Tyler was there. She laughed until her stomach hurt, her hands pressed against her body. The amused look Tyler traded with her only made the moment more important to her. He was truly enjoying hearing her laugh.

Ali wagged her finger in Ram's face. "Hey, I remember one of the other guys in the team telling me you were a cookie snatcher!"

"When I got transferred over to your team about two months later," Tyler told Ali, "that was the first thing you warned me about: to hide any baked goods from my parents. I should dig a hole and bury them or else Torres was going to sneak in and take them all."

Cara's eyes rounded. "Ram! Really? Were you stealing everyone's cookies and candy?"

Ram's cheeks grew even redder.

"Come on," Ali goaded, enjoying his discomfort, "tell them the truth!"

"Okay, okay, I'll come clean," he grumped unhappily. He looked across the table at Cara. "Yes, I had a real need of cookies and other home-baked goods. And yes, every once in a while, I'd filch a cookie or two from one of my teammates. But I never took all of 'em."

"Every once in a while?" Ali howled. She bent over, giggling so hard she couldn't speak.

Tyler snickered and slanted a glance over at Cara, who was positively shocked over this disclosure. "Ram has a serious sweet tooth," he explained. "But because he didn't take all the baked goods, we forgave him."

"Yeah, I left a few behind," Ram muttered darkly, defensive.

"Yes," Tyler said, his grin huge, "but if there were two dozen cookies, the poor SEAL who later found their stash after you'd raided it, would have only one or two left for themselves."

"Oh, Ram!" Cara said, her hand on her cheek, staring at him. "Did you really take that many?"

"Yeah," he admitted growly, squirming in his chair.

"Didn't your mom bake you cookies growing up?" Cara saw Ram's eyes shutter, nearly closed, clearly uncomfortable as he refused to meet her gaze. She felt as if she'd stepped into an unhappy memory and wished she hadn't seen the hurt on his face.

"No, not really," he managed in a strangled tone.

Everyone at the table saw that she'd asked a loaded question and that it had upset Ram. "I'm sorry," she offered, "I didn't mean to make you feel bad."

Ram recovered and shrugged. "Hey, not every family is like Tyler's or yours and Ali's, you know?"

Ali became solemn. "No, you're right, Ram."

Cara looked at Ram and then her sister, feeling as if so much were being left unsaid. The set of Ram's jaw was hard and implacable, but he wasn't angry, just . . . well . . . defensive, as if trying to hold back a lot of sad emotions. She glanced at Tyler, who was also studying Ram but saying nothing.

The table fell quiet.

Cara couldn't stand the tension. "Hey, since you're all here could you help me wrap up the Christmas sweaters I knitted for my kids after we finish our coffee?" She gave them all a hopeful look.

"Sure," Tyler said.

"Of course," Ram seconded.

Ali offered, "When we're finished with our coffee, Ram and I will clear the table. You and Tyler bring the sweaters out from your bedroom? I know where the boxes, wrapping, and ribbons are in the garage."

"Good," Cara said. She felt lighter. Was it Tyler's quiet, steady presence? She didn't know for sure, but he was the only new person in her life. She saw the happiness in his eyes. "I'm a big kid at heart," she confided in a whisper to him.

Ali grinned. "You never grew up, Cara."

She felt her face heat up as Tyler studied her, but she didn't feel threatened. Instead, there was kindness in his gaze for her. It felt good—life-affirming—and filled her with hope.

"Hey, don't pick on her, Ali," Tyler chided. "I like a woman who can be like a kid when she doesn't have to be an adult."

"Well," Ali retorted good naturedly, "that's my sister for you. You should see her with her class. You'd swear there were twenty-six kids in there, not twenty-five." She smiled, reaching out, gripping Cara's hand and giving it a fond squeeze.

"Is that true?" Tyler asked her.

"I'm afraid it is."

"Hmmm," he murmured, looking over at Ram. "Did she ever descend into this kid while you were protecting her?"

"No, not really."

"Tyler, take it from me then, she's a child when she's feeling better. The kids love her. She thinks like them and even talks with them in a language they understand."

"I'm hoping to get that part back," Cara admitted.

Ali patted her arm. "You will. It's coming."

Cara wanted her life back. Now, she was living in a before-and-after kidnapping zone.

"It will take a while," Ram reassured her. "Just take it a day at a time, Cara. You can't rush trauma that needs to be healed. Everyone has their own pace and timing with it."

"And you can't control it," she muttered. "That's what I hate most about all this."

"One of the things you can do," Tyler said, "is get back into the rhythm of the life you had before. Like knitting the sweaters for your kids, wrapping them up, and maybe taking them to the school to give to them."

She looked down at her hands, gripping the mug in front of her. "I don't know if I'm ready to go that far yet, Tyler."

"In time," he said, "you will."

"I hope so."

TYLER HELPED BRING out the boxes with Cara a little while later, taking all the sweaters to the clean kitchen table. Ram and Ali had brought in a box of wrapping and another box of ribbons, and placed them at one end of the table. Each gift box had a label with a child's name on it. He noticed the little things, such as Cara writing something special to each child. He could tell that she fiercely wanted to take back her life. The tremble in her handwriting showed him that she was probably at low tide within herself, not feeling very confident. Still, Cara persisted and he admired her courage and fortitude under the circumstances.

Stacking the boxes, he placed them on one side of the table. Ram took the chairs away, giving them room to work, and Cara brought out several pairs of scissors, tape, and colorful Christmas tags.

"These kids are going to love what you're giving them," Ali said, slipping her arm around Cara's shoulders and giving her a proud look. "I know you do this every Christmas, but this is such a wonderful present for each of them."

"I love doing it." Cara chose a roll of bright-red and green paper. "Tyler, would you wrap these five boxes in this paper? Ali, you can put the ribbon on them. Ram, could you take the name off each box and fill out a tag for it?"

"Sure," he said, gathering the tags that were in a small box. "And what are you going to do?"

She smiled a little and pointed to a card box. "I want to write each child a Christmas card and put a five-dollar bill inside." She turned to Tyler to explain.

"My kids are Hispanic and Yaqui. They're very poor. I save money out of each paycheck so I can afford to do this at Christmas for them. Five dollars might not seem like much, but to them, it's huge!"

Tyler smiled a little. "I think you're their special guardian angel."

Shrugging, feeling embarrassed, Cara said,

"Actually, those children infuse me with such joy every day that they're actually the gift that keeps on giving. They don't let me have a bad day. I might go in sometimes feeling down, but they always lift me up."

"I can see that," Tyler said, cutting the paper and sizing it for the first box.

Cara sat down at the other end of the table. "Just call out the name and I'll handwrite the Christmas card for that child?"

"You got it," Ram said.

Pretty soon, everyone was attending their jobs on this little assembly line. Cara loved all of them for helping her. There was such camaraderie between all of them. She tried not to look at Tyler too much, but he was ruggedly handsome. She wondered again if he was married. *Surely, some lucky woman had taken him to be her own.*

There was something about him that made her feel like he'd be a wonderful father. *Did he have children?* And in an assignment like this, he wasn't even with his family at Christmas. She knew Ram would leave shortly to go back to Artemis, and Ali would be leaving in mid-December as well to start her new job for the security company. They would be together celebrating Christmas back there in Virginia with the Delos and Artemis employees.

"I don't know much about bodyguards," Cara said to Tyler, "but will you get time off to go home to your family for Christmas?" She saw him look surprised.

"No. A PSD means you stay 24/7/365 or until the detail is finished."

"I'm sorry," she said. "I'm sure you'll miss your family."

"The only family Tyler has," Ram said, "is his parents who live up in Montana. They're kind of used to him not showing up on holidays."

"That's right," Tyler said. "When I come off a mission that's long term, I fly up and stay with them for a couple of weeks."

She frowned. "I thought . . . well . . . maybe you were married, had kids, and would miss Christmas with them."

"Tyler is footloose and fancy free," Ali said. "In our business, Cara, relationships aren't long term, usually."

"But yours is," she pointed out to her sister. "You and Ram will be working at the same security agency."

"Yes," Ram said, "and we'll be in the same department, which is good."

"So that means you aren't going out on missions any more, Ali?"

"Got that right," Ali said, sounding relieved. She quickly put red ribbon on the wrapped box that Tyler slid across the table to her. "I'm done with missions. Ram and I will be working in the Mission Planning Department at Artemis as part of the Central and South America Division. We'll be lending our knowledge and experience so that men or women going out into the field will be well educated to help keep them safer."

"That way," Ram told her, "people won't get killed. Artemis has some of the most sophisticated, deeply experienced combat groups of black-ops military people who have left the service and now work for them. Our combined knowledge of a given country is like gold when it comes to intel sharing. For example, Ali is a Mexico specialist. She spent years in the CIA working in there."

"And we never knew that," Cara muttered, giving Ali a dark look. "We'd see you a couple times a year, which was always great, but you could never tell us anything. Not even where you were at or what you were doing."

"It's how it had to be," Tyler said. "Everything we do in black ops is top secret or higher in the intel community."

"I don't see how you three do it—or anyone, for that matter. But if there weren't people like you protecting our country, we wouldn't enjoy what we have today."

"There are always trade-offs," Tyler agreed wryly, pushing another wrapped package toward Ali. "Freedom isn't free, Cara. It never was. I'm sure you took history in college and you know that thousands of people during the 1700s gave their lives so we could establish a democracy here. You might consider today's black-ops warriors as super patriots who are the shield between our enemies and the security of the democracy we have here in America."

Cara stopped writing in one of the cards, holding his gaze. "When Ali went into the Marine Corps that was a shock to me. I just never saw her doing something like that."

Ali grinned, pulling out a long green ribbon for another box. "I have Mama's warrior genes, Cara. You know that."

"Yes, and Mama continues to be a warrior to this day, fighting for our Yaqui nation as a steward and on the council."

"She hasn't picked up a weapon, though," Tyler noted.

"Her intelligence, voice, passion, and heart are her weapons," Ali said proudly. "Cara, there are all kinds of warriors on this planet. Not all are in the military. Mama is a peaceful warrior—and every type is important."

"I'm just glad," Cara murmured, giving her sister a loving look, "that you're going to be staying home. I don't want you to disappear from our lives so we don't know where you are. That was so hard for all of us. We worried . . ."

"I know," Ali whispered, giving her an apologetic look. "When there's evil in the world, someone has to face it down, and not all people have that kind of warrior spirit, or are willing to do it. Ram, Tyler, and I have done that."

"Yes, and no one except maybe for us, will ever know the sacrifices you all made."

"That's okay, Cara," Tyler said, wrapping the next box. "We take pride in what we do and we know we are protecting our country. That makes us feel good. It's all the payment we need."

"I was looking at your hands," Cara said, motioning toward Tyler. "You have so many scars on them—so does Ali and Ram."

Ram chuckled. "You should see the rest of our bodies, Cara. On second thought, no, you shouldn't."

"Oh, I've seen those horrible bruises and swellings on Ali," she said darkly. "Bruises that will never go away. Swelling here and there that won't go away, either."

"It's the price of admission for being a combatant," Ali told her. "It goes with the territory, Cara. We've talked about that before."

Nodding, she signed her name on a card, slipped a five-dollar bill inside and closed the envelope. "I know we have. It just scared us that you were gone somewhere in the world and we didn't know where."

"Those days are over," Ali sighed, smiling over Cara. "I'm home for good. It will be easy to catch a flight to Tucson, and you can come and pick me up at the airport. I can stay in my old room here at the house. Life is going to finally settle down for all of us," she promised, her voice suddenly thick with emotion.

"I really want that," Cara choked. "And so do Mama and Papa. We're so happy to hear you're going to work for Artemis. Now we won't worry anymore."

"It's a Christmas gift," Ali teased, "for all of us, believe me. My mission days are behind me. I'll be happy to sit at a desk."

Cara looked at Tyler. "Are you still going out on missions somewhere in the world?"

"Yes."

"Where were you before you had to babysit me, or can't you tell me?"

Tyler cut some dark-blue paper that had yellow, red, and green stars printed across it. "I was in Peru on an assignment."

"Do you like doing this? I mean, always being gone, your parents worrying about you?"

Shrugging, he said, "No, but like anyone else, I need a job. I have to pay my bills just like you do."

"Actually," Ram said, "Wyatt Lockwood, who is the head of the Mission Planning Department, is trying to talk Tyler into working in the Medical Department."

"I'm thinking about it," Tyler said.

"How old are you?" Cara asked.

"Twenty-nine."

"And his knees are almost as shot as mine,"

Ram said. "Wyatt was a SEAL, and he knows most of them leave the service around that time because their bodies are so beat up."

"You don't look beat up," Cara said.

Grinning, Tyler said, "I am. But it's more emotional than physical."

"You're a medic," Cara said, "and I'm sure you've seen some pretty awful things on the battlefield." The look in his blue eyes changed, becoming shadowed.

Nodding, Tyler pulled tape from the dispenser, quickly wrapping the box. "We've all seen things we want to forget, Cara."

Cara felt his emotional reaction, although it wasn't written in his expression. Just a heavier tone in his voice, as if he were carrying some awful, unknown load.

Ram and Ali both silently nodded, becoming somber. They had all been through so much even though Cara knew nothing about their actual missions or the dangers they had faced. The secrets they carried were burdensome judging from the looks on all their faces.

"I'm just glad," Cara told them, "that all of you are here, on US soil." She glanced over at Tyler. "At least you're not getting shot at by being here."

A slight grin tugged at one corner of his mouth. "No, this is a pretty safe assignment."

"Are you glad to be here instead of in Peru?"

"Yes." The word came out low, charged with emotion.

"Well," she offered, "I'm glad you're here, too."

"So?" Ram said, "are you okay with Tyler taking over the position as chief guard dog around here? Are you comfortable with him instead of me lumbering around underfoot?"

Nodding, she saw Tyler glance over at her, as if checking her reaction to the unexpected question. "I'm comfortable," she agreed. For a moment, she saw relief in Tyler's eyes. The tension that had been there before, had dissolved. *What did that mean?*

CHAPTER 5

December

TYLER LOOKED AT all the beautifully wrapped
Christmas gifts in the corner of the living
room. It was nine a.m. Mary and Diego had left
for work much earlier. He'd shared breakfast
with them, Cara's parents speaking in low voices
as they ate. Ram had left a few weeks ago for
Virginia to resume his job at Artemis Security; Ali
remained behind for three more weeks to ensure
her sister could continue to connect with Tyler.
Cara had sunk into a deep depression, and now
her parents looked to him for help with their
daughter as Ali continued to gently dissolve her
being here at home for Cara. It had to happen.
Otherwise, Ali would be enabling her sister, not
helping her to grow stronger by the day. He felt
deep compassion for the parents. They didn't yet
know of his psychology background, and he felt

THE HIDDEN HEART | 95

it was useful to share that nugget of information with them now—it might help them. Anyone who thought that the trauma of one family member didn't fully affect the others, was wrong. His job, as he saw it, was to quietly be there for the parents, as well as for Cara.

Mary felt that he should do "something" to encourage Cara to visit her school, and Tyler didn't disagree with her.

In the past week, he'd gotten Cara out on the street, walking to and from the end of the block where their house was located. But every time he suggested walking to her school, she balked—big time! Mary had tried to get her daughter to do the same thing but Cara adamantly refused. It was time for him to insert something new into her life.

He was out in the garage now, watching a small TV on the woodworking table. At ten a.m. the door from the kitchen opened. Turning, he saw Cara standing there. She looked exhausted, but her hair was combed and she had on a bit of makeup, which told him she was trying to look normal. The day was bright with sunshine, and it was going to get up to sixty degrees Fahrenheit.

"Hey," he called from the stool, "did you just get up, sleepyhead?" In the past week they had grown closer, but Tyler didn't necessarily see it as personal. He knew that Cara was going to lose Ali, and they were still building that bridge between one another. He saw one corner of her mouth lift a bit.

"Yes. Have you eaten?"

"I have, but I was going to come in and make a fresh pot of coffee." He slid off the wooden stool. "Interested? Want some company?" Instantly, he saw her brighten a bit. Cara looked fragile today in her black wool slacks and white, long-sleeved blouse with ruffles around the neck. Over it, she wore a bright-red shawl that she'd knitted for herself years earlier.

"That would be nice."

He liked the sudden, husky response. He was too far away to look into her eyes and try to ferret out the emotions behind her words. Then, she turned, left the door open, and disappeared inside.

Once in the kitchen, he saw Cara tie on an apron and busy herself with making some *huevos rancheros*. She had removed the shawl, and placed it over a chair at the table.

Going to the cabinet, Tyler drew down a plate, retrieved the flatware from the drawer, and set the table for her.

"How are you feeling?" he asked, as he put the coffeemaker together.

She briskly stirred the eggs in a bowl. "Depressed, but I know that it's about Ali leaving in a week. I have to go on, despite it."

He slid her a warm look. "I admire your

courage, Cara. You're a fighter and that's good."

"I don't have a choice. I woke up this morning knowing more than ever that getting well is up to me. I have to start pushing those boundaries my mind has set up to keep me stuck."

"That sounds positive." He plugged the old percolator into the wall socket. "Do you have any idea how you want to do it?"

She gave him a grim look and then poured the eggs and other ingredients into a heated, black iron skillet. "I lay there this morning thinking about that. I miss those kids more than I can tell you. Whenever I see the Christmas packages we wrapped in the corner of the living room, I hear my substitute teacher, Maria Martinez, begging me to come to the class for our annual Christmas party. My kids miss me so much." She set the bowl aside.

He saw the fear in her eyes but she was pushing it aside. Tyler silently cheered her on. "What can I do to assist you?"

She laid a warm corn tortilla on her plate, wiping her fingers off on the red apron. "I can't walk to school. Not yet. But I was wondering if you could drive me there?"

"Sure, that's a great idea. Is there another street route to your school, Cara?"

Nodding, she stirred the mixture in the skillet. "Yes, and I was thinking that when we drive there today, we take that secondary route. I didn't get kidnapped on that street, so to me, it's safer. I'm not sure I can walk it yet, though. My mind just screams at me that I'm going to get kidnapped again by Azarola."

Tyler gave her a sympathetic look. "I think you're the bravest person I've ever met, Cara. We'll take it at the pace you want. It's easy enough to drive you over to your school. What time would you like to go?"

She sighed. "I just called Maria and our principal. I want to be there at one p.m., after the children have had their lunch. I'd like to bring the gifts in at that time, too. Maria put up a Christmas tree in the room yesterday and all the kids helped decorate it." She glanced over at him. "Now, they'll all have a gift waiting for them."

"When is their last day of school before the holiday?"

"December 20th. I want to be there when they open their presents on that day. We have a wonderful celebration. I make Christmas cupcakes—which they love. After we eat, I hand out the gifts, and then everyone gets to open them."

He heard such warmth and joy in her voice as she talked about that day. "We'll make it happen."

She scooped the eggs from the skillet and into the awaiting tortilla. "I've made up my mind that by January 4th, when school reopens after the holiday, I'll be teaching there again, Tyler. I've *got* to kick this fear to the curb. It's hobbling me to the point that I feel like I'll die if I don't do this." She set the skillet aside. "Ali is right: she has to leave or she's being a crutch for me. I'm dealing with her leaving soon, too, but maybe I can refocus on what I love most: my kindergarten children. Make it positive. I just hate the anxiety when it hits me, though, Tyler." She touched her stomach. "I can barely keep it suppressed. It takes all my energy. That's why I'm so tired all the time."

"Ali, Ram, and I have the same internal fight going on as you do, Cara. We all understand what's happening with you. I might be able to help you with one part of your symptoms," he said, walking ahead and pulling a chair out for her. He then went back and retrieved the coffee and two mugs.

"Oh? Tell me while I eat, please."

Tyler poured their coffee, set the percolator on a trivet, and sat down opposite her at the table. He explained that at Artemis, their in-house physician, Dr. Dara McKinley-Culver, was treating the symptoms of anxiety, hyper-vigilance, and the feeling of threat or being stalked by invisible danger. The doctor was treating them with an adaptogen. The more he explained it to Cara, the more interested she became.

"Wait, Ali was telling me about this last

week. She said she's going in for the treatment herself, as soon as she arrives at Artemis."

"Yes. Anyone who has joined the security company must go through the process because all of us have been in combat, and we all have some level of PTSD."

"What happened to you after you took it?"

"My anxiety and all those other symptoms I just mentioned were gone in three days. It blew me away. I couldn't believe it and went back to the doc and told her. She said that was a normal amount of time for it to start taking effect."

"You said I only have to take the adaptogen for thirty days?"

"Yes. That's all. You don't take it for life, and once your symptoms stop, you'll have the sense of peace you had before the kidnapping. It basically shuts off the hormone cortisol, which has been leaking nonstop into your blood-stream."

"That sounds wonderful! You're a paramed-ic—can you help me with it?"

"I can. We'll send the results to our doctor at Artemis and Dara's assistant will send us an email detailing your diagnosis and prescription. I have a bottle of the adaptogen with me and all you have to do is follow the instructions. Hopefully, in two or three days those symptoms will be gone."

"This isn't like a tranquilizer or antidepres-sant is it, Tyler? If it is, I won't take it."

He smiled a little, watching her eat daintily. There was nothing about Cara that wasn't worth watching and absorbing. "It's not. And remember, you are on it for just thirty days, and the likelihood of ever having to take it again is very rare."

She sipped her coffee. "When can I do this?"

"How about this afternoon some time? After you see your kids." He saw more hope in her eyes. Cara was one of those rare human beings who didn't try to hide her feelings. She might be damaged and injured, but there was a core to her that shone through.

He was sure Mary and Diego's strong love and support had a lot to do with it. And Ali, being the brave woman she was, was a true role model for her younger sister. It emphasized, once again, that a healthy family environment could help a member even in the worst of circumstances.

"Yes, that's fine."

"Are you worried about me driving you to the school?"

"I'm apprehensive, but I feel better because you'll be there."

He was relieved. It had been a dicey first seven days with her, a settling-in period of adjustment for them both. But now, Cara would sometimes open up to him, treating him almost as a close confidant. Other times, she entered a dark place where it seemed no one could reach her. He understood those "dark night of the soul" moments. In fact, everyone he knew in the military had gone through this cycle often.

In Cara's case, her whole life had been shattered. She had felt safe, filled with happiness and joy from living her dream as a teacher before the kidnapping. In less than a minute, Cara's life as she knew it had ended. Now, she was trying to cobble herself back together again, still focused on her dream. Little by little, she was resurrecting it once more, following its beacon of light and hope.

She might say she was nothing like her sister, but that wasn't true. Cara had the same fierceness and passion that Ali possessed from their stalwart mother. But now, Cara had to redirect those emotions, and focus on that dream, so she could once again move forward. In Tyler's opinion, she was doing it quickly. He hadn't met many people, with the exception of Ram Torres, who possessed such a strong survival mechanism. Cara was lucky to have a wonderful family from whom she had inherited that same tough, deep core, as Ali.

CARA TRIED TO push her anxiety away as she slid out of Tyler's SUV and stepped into the warm afternoon sunshine. She had just arrived at the yellow stucco kindergarten and grade school, which sat behind a tall black wrought-iron fence. He got out of the vehicle and sized up the area. The street was small and quiet, the school nestled in a Hispanic neighborhood.

Cara knew to wait for him as he rounded the vehicle and pressed in the numbers on the pad to open the gate so she could enter the school grounds. Green Palo Verde trees were scattered across the gold-colored, fine gravel on either side of the red tile walk.

"Nervous?" he asked, walking at her side after locking the gate behind them. Tyler had made it his business to contact the principal and get a map of the school. He'd placed a copy in his smart phone and let her and the staff know that Cara would be coming back to see the children today. Her children had been told she'd been ill and they accepted that explanation without question.

He'd already memorized the layout of her classroom, the exit/entrance points, the windows, and many other items on a security detail's list. He would not tell Cara about this because he wanted her to focus on getting back on her feet.

Cara looked around, feeling wistful. "Actually, I'm just eager to see my kids." The sunlight warmed her, so she had taken off the red knit shawl and replaced it with a brightly colored red, orange, and yellow scarf, draped elegantly around her shoulders. She touched her small gold earrings, wanting to look the same as she had before the kidnapping. "First, I want to see the principal and get some help carrying in those gifts for the kids," she said.

Nodding, Tyler followed her. They went through two bulletproof security doors connected with the main office. After proper identification, they were allowed through the entrance. The halls were empty because the classes were in session. This was a kindergarten through sixth grade school. Tyler had done his homework, finding that 60% of the children were Hispanic, and the rest were Native American, Caucasian, African American, and a few Asian children. It was what he termed a "melting pot region" of south Tucson. The principal, Jody Campbell, was in her fifties, a warm administrator who spoke four languages and reminded him a lot of Cara when it came to enthusiasm and passion. Now, he opened the door to the principal's office.

All the staff, mostly women, cried out with joy when they saw Cara. He stood back, watching as four of them rushed around the counter and threw their arms around her. She melted with joy, smiling, crying, and clinging to her friends. He wished he could do that for her: hold her, let her cry, wrap his arms around her, letting her know that there was safety there, with him.

More and more, he wanted her on a personal level, fighting the desire hourly. As a professional, he couldn't get personally involved with her— and yet, he knew it was happening, no matter what he did to tamp down the attraction. He would definitely have to hide what was in his heart. After all, Cara couldn't handle a relationship right now on top of trying to get back to teaching. He had been around her enough, and had had serious, searching conversations with her at the house to know her whole life was about teaching, family, and her children. She was just built that way and it appealed mightily to him.

When the group finally eased away from Cara, she wiped her eyes, giving him a watery smile, she then introduced him to everyone. None of the women, thankfully, let on that he had been here at the school days before. That was their secret. Everyone loved Cara, that was a given. She was just one of those bright flowers in a field that all gazes gravitated to first.

What would it be like to love this woman? Take her to his bed? Touch her? Feel her hands skimming and memorizing his body? Responding when she kissed him back?

Focusing on the immediate situation, Tyler followed Cara around the desk and walked down the hall to the principal's large office. He could hardly wait to see Cara and her children meet after she'd been gone for more than two months.

CARA FOUGHT TO hold her emotions in check as she entered the only classroom she'd ever known. Maria had the children standing on either side of her. The children all had their eyes closed. She had told them that they were going to get a big surprise. Entering softly on her tiptoes after Tyler had opened the door, Cara waved hello to Maria, who had the biggest smile on her face. Her charges were antsy, moving on one foot and then the other. They were so excited they were barely able to keep from peeking. She felt tears come to her eyes. These were *her* children.

She felt guilty for having abandoned them, but Maria was a wonderful teacher and Cara knew she had lovingly taken care of all twenty-five of them in her absence. She felt Tyler move up behind her and felt his silent embrace. How could he feel that she was near tears? Looking up and across her shoulder, she saw him smile down at her. It was the deep caring in his eyes that touched her heart as never before.

How many times had she awakened in the morning, thinking of him. He was a quiet, unobtrusive shadow in her life; someone she had come to rely on as much as she had Ram. Tyler's sensitivity and kindness was always just below his surface and never failed to touch her deeply. He was so much like her father, Diego.

Turning, she gave Maria the signal.

"Okay, kids, open your eyes!" Maria called excitedly.

Cara was at the other end of the large room. All the desks had been pushed to the sides, leaving the polished oak floor shining beneath the sunlight, a wide avenue between the two teachers. Cara saw the children's faces, collective shock on all of them. And then, when they realized she had come back, they squealed with delight, calling her name, and then charging toward her.

She laughed and held out her arms to them. The five-year-old boys raced up first, throwing their arms around her hips and her waist, jumping up and down, huge smiles on their faces. The little girls came next, calling out to her, their tiny arms open as they flew down the length of the room toward her.

Swamped with emotion, Cara leaned over cuddling all of them around her, unable to embrace all of them, but she tried. They were like live, wriggling, excited puppies, ecstatic to see her once again.

Tyler stood back watching, warmth flooding throughout him. The twenty-five children were a living mass, constantly moving around Cara, their hands touching hers, their faces shining as they looked adoringly up at her.

But it was the tender expression on Cara's face that totaled him. He knew what she'd survived and knew the courage it took to get this far into her recovery. He recalled a mission he was on in Toulouse, France, following a subject who had slipped into the Notre-Dame de la Daurade, a beautiful Gothic church. Tyler had followed the man to an alcove, where six rows of wooden benches were located. There, above them, was a black Madonna clothed in turquoise-blue fabric with shining silver stars throughout it.

It was only when his subject sat down in the first row, head bowed in prayer, that Tyler got a good look at the Madonna's serene, sculpted features. Now, he watched another Madonna—Cara. Her cheeks were bright red, her lips smiling, her laughter mingling with the cries from her children. There was such serenity in her expression, such joy radiating outward from her like sunlight flooding the entire room.

Tyler knew there were some people, both men and women, who were made to be parents. He thought of his own parents, and then of Mary and Diego Montero. He knew how fortunate he was to have parents who had truly loved raising a child, actually celebrating the unique individual the child was becoming throughout the years.

Soon, two janitors arrived with dollies, the Christmas packages stacked on each. The children oohed and ahhed, jumping up and down, knowing that Cara had knitted each of them a brand new sweater. However, Tyler noticed they didn't leave her side to run over to the Christmas tree to see where their packages were being placed beneath it. No, those kids wanted to be close to her, smiling up at her, touching her hand, her arm. Some of the little girls held on to the side of her trousers, as if needing her physical contact. Their languages like a little United Nations—a blend of Spanish, the Yaqui language, and English whizzing around among them.

Cara was laughing, leaning over, and kissing each of them on the head, making sure that every child felt the fullness of her love.

Tyler remained the shadow in the room, watching the noisy, tumultuous occasion. He'd never seen Cara so alive, wondering if this was how she had been before the kidnapping. If it was, she stunned him and took his breath away. Her lips were always drawn in a sincere smile, her face mobile as she interacted with each child.

The looks on those tiny faces after getting officially hugged by Cara sent his heart off in an ache of old memories. Once his marriage had been happy, at least the first three months of it when he was stateside, before he went overseas on deployment once more. He'd never been happier. *Until now.* It was as if Cara had somehow boosted him into unknown realms he never knew existed until this moment. She was magic.

He watched the door open as the principal came in with two other female teachers. In their hands were trays of cookies and cold cartons of milk. The children went into a frenzy, yipping and dancing around over their good fortune. He noticed the cookies were either green or red, with lots of silver Christmas sprinkles. He smiled as they settled down with one graceful gesture from Cara. They wanted to please her so badly.

The children sat in a circle around her, legs crossed, expressions radiant. Cara asked the girls to go forward first and choose one cookie of their choice and pick up a carton of milk. Then, they were to sit down on a big, red wool blanket that the two janitors had just unrolled and placed near the Christmas tree.

Cara disentangled herself from several little girls, urging them to get their cookies and she followed behind them to the trays. Tyler was pleasantly surprised when she walked over to him and said, smiling, "For you."

"Thanks," he murmured, touched by her sensitivity.

"Are you doing okay, Tyler?"

He laughed. "Yeah, this is quite a celebration, isn't it?" He saw the sparkle in her eyes and suddenly, his gaze dropped to her lips—that was a mistake. Tyler didn't want to go there right now. In the torrid dreams he had on some nights, yes. *But not now.*

She stood beside him, nibbling on her green cookie. "It's a wonderful welcome back to what I love to do most."

"Are the kids this high-energy all the time?"

Chuckling, she said, "Yes. We make sure to get them out for recesses and we also have physical games in the classroom. Children are born to move and the first twelve years of their life they should be off exploring, being physically active. We make sure they get plenty of fresh air, sunshine, and lots of exercise every day."

"They seem to like you." He teased, grinning, and saw her face become tender as she regarded her children, now sitting on the blanket, gobbling their cookies with gusto.

"It's a love fest every day for me. I know all the parents, their struggles, and their issues with their children. I see it as a positive challenge, and the principal and the teachers try to help families in need of counseling, or food from our local pantry, or help paying their utilities bills."

"Did Mary inaugurate you and Ali into helping others when you were kids?"

"Mama always took us to work with her. She works with Pima County officials as well as the reservation people and knows all the contacts who help struggling families. I think it rubbed off on us."

"I think you're doing great. The kids are a lot of fun to watch."

"Thanks," she said, touching her cheek, feeling the heat rise in it. "Does it remind you of you as a little boy?" she grinned impishly.

He returned the smile. "Yeah, a lot. I was a handful, too."

"I want to sit with my kids for a moment, and then we'll go, okay?"

"Just say the word. Go have fun."

CARA WAS EXHAUSTED, but elated, when Tyler took her home. She stole a glance in his direction. "You seemed to really enjoy being with me at the school."

He walked her into the kitchen, taking off the jacket that he routinely wore when out in public to conceal his weapon. "I like kids."

"Not all men do," she said, going into the kitchen.

"I don't think all men and women were cut out to be parents, either," he said, following her. It wasn't an indictment against them, simply an observation and nothing more. She was busy making them a fresh pot of coffee and liked the ease between them.

"I don't disagree." She sighed and plugged the percolator in. Turning, she rested her hands on the counter, looking up at this big man. He wasn't as heavy as Ram Torres, but he had muscle, no doubt. "You said you had a happy family like ours?"

"Yes. I was a wild child, but my parents never once hit me, yelled at me, or did anything close to the abuse that I see in my job when on missions."

"Firm love is the order of the day," she agreed, smiling a little. "Loving firmness. Sometimes tough love. It's all about setting boundaries."

"My parents had this idea that children had to grow into whatever they wanted to be. They always told me I could be whatever I dreamed of being, and supported me in anything that drew my interest."

"Did you dream of being a SEAL?"

He came and rested his hips against the counter, leaving several feet between them. "No. But what I did dream of was being of service and helping people. My father is a gemstone miner, so he was not like the normal dad. There are lots of sapphires to be mined in the Rocky Mountains around Philipsburg, Montana. When I was old enough, I would go out into the forest and work with him at his mining claim. I loved it, and I loved being outside."

"I didn't know that," Cara said, tilting her head. "Was he able to make money at it?"

"Yes. But he worked from daylight to dusk out at his mining claim after the winter snow melted. He had a window of about four months before the snows came and buried his claim in six to ten feet of the white stuff for seven months of the year."

"And your mother? What does she do?"

He gave her a roguish smile. "She's a school teacher just like you. She teaches first through sixth grades in Philipsburg."

"Oh!" Cara stared at him, stunned. "Really? Your mother is a school teacher?" Joy coursed through her. No wonder Tyler seemed at ease around all those noisy, happy children.

"Yeah." He laughed a little. "I grew up taking trays of cookies and cupcakes to school for her, too. Kind of felt good to get back in the saddle on that one."

"That's incredible, Tyler. I thought . . . well . . . I thought you might hate the noise, the kids running around . . ."

"Not me," Tyler said softly. "I see kids as little flower buds, and as they grow up in a family, they're starting to open the petals of who they are, as individuals, during that time. And the idea of a flower opening wasn't mine, but my mom's way of seeing children. She'd draw a sunflower on the whiteboard and put a petal on it and tell the children that today, they were going to learn something that would help them grow in that new direction."

She studied him, hearing the low emotion in his voice, the love he held for his mother. "That's a wonderful visual! I think if it's all right with your mom, I'm going to start using that too. Kids will love it! I can make them think that each petal is a mystery that's about to reveal something about each of them. Like an ongoing treasure hunt, mining for who they are and what they love to do."

Without thinking, she threw her arms around his shoulders, giving him a hard hug. He smelled male, a faint scent of the soap he'd used, the same one her father used! For a split second, he froze. And then he relaxed and she released him, dazed by that quiet strength that was so much a part of him. "You've been a gift to me, Tyler," she whispered, resting against the counter once more. "I thought . . . well . . . I thought you'd never measure up to Ram, or the emotional harbor of peace he gave me, but I was wrong."

She gave a small shrug, seeing the shock of her hugging him leave his eyes, replaced with one of tenderness that she knew for certain was just for her. "I just never expected to find a second man with kindness in him who would be my bodyguard. Ram is gruff, but he's kind beneath. He helped me through the worst of my weeks after I got home."

"Ram is like a rough gemstone on the outside, but he's a good man," Tyler pointed out quietly. "I can see why you trusted him with your life."

"I trust you too, Tyler," she said, searching his eyes. She compressed her lips, studying him.

"That's good to know." He cleared his throat. "I was hoping maybe someday you could get there."

"I saw the children who came up to you, curious. The first thing you did was crouch down so you weren't so tall and threatening to them." She saw his cheeks grow ruddy, his eyes narrowing slightly upon her. "They trusted you from the first time they saw you. Kids have phenomenal knowing and it's instinctive. I almost cried when several of the boys ran over to you, holding up their wrapped gifts for you to see."

Tyler smiled tentatively. "I could tell you were close to tears."

"I'm far more emotional than I used to be. I can barely control it sometimes. Will that go away after I get on this adaptogen?"

"I don't know. I know it takes away the anxiety and gives a person their old sense of peace and calm back. Maybe ask Ali when she goes through the regimen once she starts to work at Artemis?"

Nodding, Cara wanted to say so much more, but felt it wasn't prudent right now. "I loved finding out that your dad is a gem miner. Maybe at dinner tonight we can talk more about your family, okay? I'd love to know them, because I think they're special."

"Sure," he said. "I told Mary I'd do the cooking tonight. I know Ali is going out with some of her friends for the evening, so I thought I'd pitch in."

Laughing a little, Cara said, "My mother always involves everyone who stays with us. Could you use a little help?"

"Sure, all I can get," he laughed. "When I told her it was going to be beans and wieners, she didn't look too happy about my culinary choice."

"Oh, geez," Cara said, touching her brow, smiling. "No, my mother loves her native foods or Latin foods. Let me help you make some chicken enchiladas tonight, may I? I know we have soft tortillas and some leftover chicken from yesterday. We'll whip up something together."

"Phew, you just saved my life, Cara. Thanks," he teased. Her laughter felt like warm honey being poured into his heart.

CHAPTER 6

December 20

CARA COULD BARELY hold on to her emotions as Tyler helped her bring in the cupcakes they had made for her school children. Maria was there, helping with the children, all wriggling madly in their chairs. Cara watched them, listening to their high voices like a flock of chirping birds.

She had come back twice since her first visit, acclimating herself to "Cara 2.0," as Tyler teasingly called it. Her struggles to recreate the teacher all the children loved was supporting her immensely. He'd told her the other day over breakfast that she was now 2.0 and she agreed: a new and improved version of her old self. Cara had started this Christmas bounty for her kindergarten class last year and it was the highlight of the year for them. She wasn't about to disappoint them. Ali had left already, but it hadn't caused Cara to dive into depression, such was the progress she was making on healing herself.

Tyler brought in the last tray and once again became a quiet, shadowy presence in the back of the room, near the door. He hoped that his presence was a small part of the reason for Cara's progress. The children had gotten used to him being around and the boys, especially, liked coming over to ask him about who he was and why he was here whenever Cara arrived to the schoolroom. She was glad Tyler lied and told them that he was a good friend of her family and was here on a long visit with them. The children accepted it without any question, to her relief.

Her emotions seesawed between the thrill of preparing her Christmas gift party for the children and the closeness that was clearly deepening between her and Tyler. How little she realized that the day she'd spontaneously thrown her arms around his shoulders, hugging him in thanks, it had subtly changed the trajectory of their relationship.

She wasn't a stranger to having a man in her life, although Colin had disappeared after she'd been kidnapped. There was nary a word from him, not that she'd tried to contact him, either. Those who had stood at her side since then had been her unwavering parents, her sister, Ram

Torres, and now, Tyler. Her father had never been in the military but his love, his support of her through the ups and downs, never wavered—and neither had her mother, her sister, Ram, or Tyler. They had all accepted her symptoms as a natural matter of course, which was helping her to put them into perspective, as well.

The children were excited today, their voices high pitched, the boys positively restless, squirming around in their chairs and the girls smiling but patient, watching her every move. First came the Christmas cupcakes. Maria took one side of the room and Cara took the other. She and Tyler had worked two days on decorating these huge, white frosted chocolate cupcakes. They'd had a lot of fun and shared a lot of laughter during that time, which filled Cara's heart with even more warmth toward him.

Tyler didn't lose a shred of his masculinity when she tied a red apron around his waist. Making thick icing, coloring it, getting it into a squeezable tube, all held potential for lots of mishaps, trials, and errors—but it had been fun. She loved that Tyler knew the children now, and he seemed just as excited about decorating each cupcake differently with her. She would forever hold these memories in her heart.

She laid a red or green napkin in front of her charges, daintily taking a heavily decorated cupcake and placing one in front of each of them.

Just the way their small, slender fingers wrapped around the dessert, almost reverently, made her feel good. The *ooh*s and *aah*s as the children surveyed their special cupcakes echoed their constant surprise. She watched their eyes grow huge as they carefully surveyed their creative dessert. One had Frosty the Snowman on it, another, Rudolph the Red-Nosed Reindeer, and another, a decorated Christmas tree. It was almost a shame to eat and destroy the careful artwork she and Tyler had created together. It had been Tyler who had taken photos of the cupcakes for her, saying that such art should never be forgotten. She'd laughed, but she was glad he'd done it.

Other cupcakes had stars in a night sky, a camel with a wise man standing next to the animal, a holly wreath, several candles with flames, and a snowy hill with a child on a sled. Tyler proved to be a perfectionist, very careful, and very good at decorating. He said he'd gotten that skill from being a SEAL and paying attention to every last detail. They'd had a good laugh over that, too.

She couldn't stop smiling these days. Sometimes, she'd lift her head after delivering one of those cupcakes to a child, to see Tyler watching her from afar. She wasn't innocent, and she knew when a man was interested in her—and Tyler was, no question about that. Since that hug, he'd seemed more withdrawn though, and she wondered if she'd breached some unknown protocol between them. Maybe a bodyguard wasn't supposed to be hugged? She didn't know. But meeting his crystalline blue gaze, she felt her entire body and heart respond to him. There was a slight smile hovering around his mouth—the very same mouth she'd fantasized about since he'd come to guard her. Sometimes, she found herself wanting to take her fingertip and slowly, gently, trace the outline of its contours.

And of course, the next thought she couldn't escape was, what would it be like to kiss him? Would he be rough? Tender? Hungry? Cara didn't know, but she wanted to find out. She often saw him watching her, but it made her feel good, desired, and healthily attractive.

She'd found out the difference between positive and negative attraction. If Tyler looked at her, it felt right to her body and mind. But when one of those drug soldiers had stared at her like a salivating hyena, terror had shot through her, and she wanted to scream and escape.

Maddeningly, Tyler's expression was always unreadable except when they were alone. Out in public, as he'd told her, his game face was in place. He didn't want anyone reading his expressions or being able to know what he was thinking. Still, as she met his eyes right now, his smile grew broader, and he gave her a nod of acknowledgement. It had been so subtle no one else had noticed but her. Her lower body was growing achy over those burning looks he'd shoot her from time to time. This was the look of a man who wanted his woman.

As she handed out the last of her cupcakes, she gave him a merry smile, turned, and went to the front desk. She had a surprise for Tyler. Picking up the last cupcake she'd hidden from him, she walked the length of the room to where he stood.

"This is for you," she said, holding it out to him along with a napkin.

Tyler straightened and looked down. He saw a pink heart with a white star in the center of it, surrounded by swirls of red frosting. "Thanks," he murmured. "I didn't know they had hearts at Christmas!" He looked up, meeting her winsome smile, and saw how her eyes danced with life. "Did you forget and think it was Valentine's Day?"

She laughed and took a step back. "No, it's just how I feel about you." Her voice lowered, a slight quaver as she looked up, holding his shocked gaze. "Whether you know it or not, Tyler, you've helped me heal in so many ways. I thought Ram had done a lot for me—and he did, but you picked up where he left off."

She barely touched his shaven cheek. "You've made me want to live again, and that's a priceless gift. That certainly deserves more than a cupcake, but I know you'll understand and accept my words into your heart." She turned and quickly walked back to where Maria stood.

Tyler stared down at the huge cupcake in his palm. His cheek tingled where Cara's soft fingertips had barely grazed his flesh. Her words were stunning and her honesty, gut-wrenching. She had said all the things he'd been wanting to share with her from his own heart—his hidden heart. And yet, he had to maintain that same veneer, even if every part of him wanted to let her know his feelings for her, the dreams he had of them together. When she turned and walked away, he watched her swaying hips and swallowed hard, knowing he could not have her—at least, not yet.

Cara gave the word for the kids to dig in and eat their cupcakes. Maria had already dispensed cold cartons of milk to each child, and for a few minutes, all that could be heard was children making happy sounds as they tore the silver foil off from around their cupcake. Frosting smeared their noses and cheeks, their tiny mouths full of bits of chocolate cupcake.

It was a golden moment for her as she watched, feeling tears prick the backs of her eyes. Cara pushed them away because today she did not want her children to see her crying. No, this was a day of celebration, not sadness.

As she stood there, she realized more than ever that life was precious. One moment she had been deliriously happy with her existence as she walked home to her parents' house; and the next second, she'd been kidnapped, a needle jabbed into her shoulder. She'd lost consciousness and woke up in a van, terrified, unable to figure out what had happened or where she was.

Cara tried to push that memory away because it had no business arising on this wonderfully happy day. A new sense of gratitude flooded through her, an acknowledgement that life was fragile and that one should find joy by loving every moment, because there might not be another. Maybe it was the adaptogen that Dr. Dara McKinley-Culver had her on, the anxiety had left her three days after taking it. Since then, a new and welcome peace lived within her.

With the anxiety gone, so was the hyper-vigilance, and the paranoia about the drug lord coming after her again had also disappeared. This amazing substance had freed her up to get back onto the tracks of her life as she'd been before that incident that had threatened to change her forever.

She saw Tyler nibbling at the cupcake from beneath. He wasn't eating the frosted top. *Why?* Smiling, she shook her head. Who knew what thoughts motivated her dear bodyguard. When he had his game face in place, all she could do was try to pick up nuances of what he might really be feeling. *Why on earth was he not eating the frosting? That was the best part!* Cara watched as her charges dutifully began wiping off their messy faces and sticky fingers with those huge paper napkins.

Their little faces showed even more excitement now that they knew what was coming next. Cara and Maria would go to the Christmas tree and read the tag on each gift, and then take it to the child to whom it belonged. Once the packages were distributed, they got to tear them open and see what kind of sweater Cara had knitted for them. The excitement was palpable in the room. Maria brought a small wastebasket around to each long table, taking the napkins and cleaning up each desk of crumbs so the surface was clean and ready for the gift to come.

One by one, Maria and Cara brought out the individually wrapped gifts. Each child struggled mightily not to open it. Rather, they eagerly ran their tiny hands around and around the colorful Christmas paper, curling the ends of the ribbons around their index fingers. The girls always touched the fancy bows, the boys turning their boxes upside down, shaking it near their ear, and trying somehow to see through it to look at the color of the sweater Cara had made for them.

Unable to stop from smiling, Cara knew each of her children as if they were her own. She knew each one's favorite color. And she always knitted a symbol into the sweater that meant something to that child. Her love was overflowing now as she gave them the signal to open their gifts.

In seconds, wrapping paper was being ripped open, fragments flying through the air like confetti throughout the room. The boys tore off ribbons while the girls patiently untied the knot, savoring the silky ribbon and gently untangling it from the box, laying it aside. Cara laughed, and so did Maria. The boys took no prisoners. The girls wanted to save the ribbons and not tear into the pretty giftwrap. She cast a look in Tyler's direction and her heart melted with the expression on his face. He was just as touched as she was.

There were cries of surprise as the boys yanked open the boxes to reveal another layer of red tissue paper wrapped around their gift. That got torn off in seconds, too. She wished she could watch all twenty-five of their faces as they saw their new sweater for the first time, but it was impossible. Manuel, six-years-old, held his black sweater up with a palomino-colored horse head on the front of it. His two front teeth were missing, and he was grinning from ear to ear. Cara was lost in a sea of children's cries, yips, and shouts as they each held their soft, new sweater in their hands. The girls had lighter, pastel colors while the boys' sweaters were darker, more conservative colors. But they all loved the individual symbol that Cara had knitted for each of them.

For Isabella, there was a stethoscope because she yearned to become a doctor. For Camilia, there was her gray kitty cat with a white blaze and white paws. And for Luciana, who dreamed of being a writer, Cara had knitted a pen and paper on the front of her bright red sweater.

The boys quickly pulled their sweaters over their heads, proudly tugging them down into place. The girls ran their small hands over the angora yarn, marveling at how soft it felt, holding it up, making happy sounds over the symbol Cara had awarded to each of them.

"Okay," Maria called, clapping her hands, "time to put them on! We need a group picture! Ms. Montero has brought her camera. Come up to the front of the room. Tall children in back, shorter ones in the front!"

Cara walked to the rear of the room where Tyler was standing. Nearby on a table was her purse and camera. She smiled. "Well, what do you think? Isn't this wonderful?"

"Sure is. Never seen anything like it."

She eyed the top of the cupcake that was sitting on a napkin near her purse. "Aren't you going to eat it?"

"No . . . not yet. Just want to kind of savor it for the moment."

She saw intention in his eyes as she reached for her camera. There was thoughtfulness in his look and something else so deep that she couldn't begin to fathom what it might be. But whatever it was, it made her feel special—and desired.

"Better watch out," she laughed, "or one of those boys, probably Santiago, will spot that uneaten part of your cupcake and steal it out from under your nose."

He laughed. "I'm watching it, believe me."

Turning, she nodded and walked to the middle of the room where Maria was getting the children formed into a half circle, two deep. They all looked like pretty little meadow flowers, proud and happy in their new, larger sweaters. The boys kept turning and showing the other boys on either side of them the symbols on their sweaters. The girls were moving their small fingers up and down across the fuzzy, downy yarn, marveling at the colors, the weave, and how pretty their symbols were.

"Okay," Cara called in English, "let's try to stand quietly. I don't want your face or your sweater blurred."

Instantly, the children hushed, fully focused on her as she knelt down on one knee of her dark-brown trousers and lifted the camera up.

"Smile," she called, laughing.

Instantly, twenty-five faces bloomed in such wide smiles that it dazzled Cara. She clicked the camera three times. The rest of their Christmas gift was going to be two-fold: first, she would have copies of the best photo taken of the group developed at the local drugstore. Then, she would take an individual photo of each child standing in front of a white background and it, too, would be turned into a photo. Only this time, Cara would use her own money to have copies made for each set of parents to put that new photo in their wallets or purses—each child would get a small, wallet-sized photo of themselves, too. A larger, five-by-seven photo would be framed and given to the family, where they could put it in a special place for all to see.

Cara would spend the next hour carefully taking photos from the waist up of each child. And then, when done with the photo session, a tray of sugar cookies that Tyler had personally decorated would be offered to them. After that, they would leave school for their holiday vacation.

TYLER ENJOYED BEING a quiet shadow in Cara's life. He had literally watched her bloom over the past few weeks. Getting to decorate the Christmas cupcakes had been another happy turn in their relationship. He'd never laughed so hard or as long as when she'd tell a story about one of her children. For the first time, he was getting to see the real Cara Montero, not the wounded woman they'd found in that drug lord's villa in the Sierra Madres of Mexico.

Ali had told him that Cara had always had a boyfriend and now, he could see why. The woman he saw today in the classroom was stunning in every possible way. He wrestled with his selfish side, the side that wanted to let her know how much she meant to him, to share a moment where she felt safe and loved—but he could do nothing like that.

That evening, in the living room, the whole family gathered to decorate the newly arrived Christmas tree. The day before, Tyler, Cara, and Diego had gone up to Mt. Lemmon in the Santa Catalina Mountains north of Tucson. The mountain was over nine-thousand feet in altitude, the tallest one in the chain. Diego had gotten a permit to chop down a tree for Christmas, and Cara had gone with them because Tyler could not leave her alone as a PSD.

Tyler had watched with pleasure as father and daughter laughed, smiled, and looked at dozens of trees along one slope of the mountain. He had wanted to join them, but that wasn't his job.

It was Cara's breathy laughter, running in and around the trees, her arms out, fingers brushing the greenery as she skipped by them, snow flying off the limbs like magical fairy dust, that had made his heart yearn to be running at her side.

She was more childlike today. Yesterday, she had played the role of a mother to her children in her classroom. How many other wonderful sides did Cara have that he hadn't yet encountered? Since she'd taken the adaptogen and was no longer run by the anxiety, he was watching her change almost miraculously before his eyes.

Ali had told him in a Skype call from Virginia, that Cara was usually the cheerful one in their family. Of course, that hadn't shown up until very recently. He looked forward to his weekly calls with Ali and Ram in the late hours of night, letting them know how Cara was doing. Ali was very excited because she said the "old" Cara was resurfacing once again, and she had been right.

Every day Tyler watched the woman who had hidden in the shadows, slowly begin to emerge in the light of day. It truly was like watching a seedling rise from the ground, and then grow, forming a bud and one petal at a time, opening and revealing who she really was when not avalanched by that soul-destroying anxiety.

Tyler watched from the couch, where he sat near Cara, as Diego brought out a medium-sized cardboard box marked "*Navidad*," which meant "Christmas." Setting it down on the kitchen table, the man straightened and gestured for him to come over.

"We must be men and string these lights so Mary and Cara can begin to trim the tree," he said.

In the evening hours, Tyler wore an ankle pistol hidden beneath his jeans. That way, the family wasn't always starkly reminded of why he was with them. "I think we can do that," he told Diego, returning his smile.

"Ali and Cara, as children, just loved having lots and lots of lights on the tree," Diego told him wistfully, opening the box and picking up a carefully wrapped group, then giving Tyler the other end. "I swear," he said, shaking his head, "I think if we did not have the money for a tree, as *niñas*, all I would have had to do was buy lots of strings of lights, decorate their doorways and windows, and they still would have been in heaven."

Tyler saw Cara with Mary pulling out a number of decorations and setting them around the box. "My parents had planted a small Scotch pine out in our yard, not too far from our picture window. Every Christmas my dad and I took waterproof lights out and decorated it."

Diego helped him carry the lights to the five-foot tree sitting in the corner of the living room. "That way, you did not kill a tree," he pointed out.

"Yes. My parents are very eco-conscious."

"But where did they put your gifts?" he wondered, getting a step stool and starting at the top of the evergreen.

"My mother loves ceramics," Tyler said, moving the string around the tree. "She made a two-foot high Christmas tree complete with lights. We always sat it on an antique Queen Anne desk that had come down a hundred years through my mother's side of the family. It sat in a corner, near our flagstone fireplace. All gifts were placed around it."

"I see," Diego said, ladling out more of the string to Tyler. "Another way to celebrate *Niño* Christ's birth. A very beautiful and practical way."

"Yes, it was." His family wasn't very religious, mostly a mixture of beliefs. He liked working with Diego because the man was the epitome of kindness, sensitive to others, and such a hard worker for his family. In many ways, his own father, Bill, was similar. Diego was the manager of a pecan orchard near Marana, Arizona. His father dug his hands into the earth to make a living discovering sapphires in the rough. Both men were of the earth: tall, sinewy, and deeply tanned because they were out in the elements and weather daily.

Diego brought over the second string and they wound it around and around the tree. He glanced toward the kitchen where the women were laughing and chatting. Then, bending down, Tyler plugged in the string and the whole tree lit up. He straightened, his hands on his hips as he and Diego regarded their handiwork. Diego slid him a glance, his dark brown eyes glittering with laughter. "You see?" He waved his hand at the tree. "Did I not tell you? This tree looks like it belongs on the Las Vegas strip!"

Chuckling, Tyler said, "Yeah, for sure. I don't believe I've ever seen a tree that looked this gaudy."

"You know children. Bright, pretty lights are awe-inspiring to them. I wish you could have seen our daughters when they had their first Christmas tree." He placed his hand on his long-sleeved blue and white plaid shirt, over his heart. "Mary and I had tears in our eyes because we did not know they would be so touched by the lights. Ali was five and Cara was three at the time. From then on, they begged, pleaded, and cried for lots of lights. I really believe the lights outnumber the bulbs they will hang shortly."

"Do you know of a woman who doesn't like bling and glitter?"

Diego laughed heartily. "*Sí, sí,* that is true!"

As the women came over, praising both men, Diego took Tyler by the arm and guided him into the kitchen.

"Time for our ceremonial Yaqui hot choco-late," he told Tyler, who was leaning against the counter, watching the women trim the tree.

"I like family traditions," Tyler said. "Is there anything I can do to help, Diego?"

"No, no, just stand and watch. This is Mary's

recipe and she's sworn me to secrecy, but you can observe." His eyes gleamed. "My dear wife is proud of her heritage. And this recipe comes from the Aztecs." He brought up a pan and set it on the gas stove. Quickly, he gathered the necessary ingredients. "Every Christmas I make hot chocolate while they decorate. Then we all have a cup of it at the table and admire the beauty of our tree."

"Sounds good," Tyler murmured, watching him take some ground vanilla, and chocolate from cacao plants, both originating from Central America. He added cinnamon from Sri Lanka, ground cloves, salt, brown sugar and some secret ingredient in an unmarked jar. As Diego began stirring the concoction in milk, the scent became intoxicating.

"Ummm . . . smells good, too," Tyler added.

"Mary has already made us some cinnamon chocolate bark," he said, pointing to a platter filled with dark-chocolate pieces. "There are pistachios, cashews, dried dates, and cranberries mixed into an Aztec dark chocolate from central Mexico. I am happy that you will be sharing our ceremony, Tyler." Diego hesitated, and then said in a low tone, "My daughter cares very much for you. I don't know if you realize that or not?"

Heart thudding once, he saw the kindness in Diego's eyes as he regarded him while stirring the chocolate. "I didn't know that, sir."

"My youngest daughter," he sighed, shaking his head, "was once a dreamer and an idealist." His black brows fell as he stirred the mixture. "With the kidnapping, she changed dramatically and we were both shocked by her transformation. Ali and Ram kept us from going *loco* over it because we didn't understand about trauma."

"She's gone through a lot," Tyler agreed. "And people can change after such an experience."

"My wife and I would drive over to the Dove of the Desert, Mission San Xavier del Bac. We go to mass there because of the beauty of it, the ancient history of this mission, and the feeling of peace that surrounds it. We went to mass weekly and prayed for Cara, prayed to God to help her. Our local Catholic church was helping, too. They arranged a prayer circle of parishioners after mass to pray for Cara's healing, as well. My wife's tribe performed a sacred ceremony for her." He took a clean spoon, dipped it into the steaming mixture, and blew on it a moment before tasting it.

"*Bueno*," Diego murmured, placing the spoon in the sink. "It's just about ready."

"Prayers are always welcome," Tyler agreed, watching Mary and Cara. They were tittering excitedly like two lively, beautiful birds as they hung colorful bulbs on the limbs around the tree. "Does Cara know this secret recipe's ingredients?"

"No. Perhaps we will let her know, but that will be in the future. Right now, since you gave her that medicine she has begun returning to her old self, the sweet daughter we knew before. I think you can see the changes, eh?"

"I can. It's remarkable. Almost a night and day difference."

"Now we know what trauma does to a human being," Diego said sadly. "We have firsthand knowledge and I do not wish this on anyone. Ever. And we didn't realize Ali had it too, this awful PTSD. But she handled it very differently than Cara."

"Because Ali is a trained military combatant," Tyler explained. "It protects us up to a point when we're caught in a traumatic situation. Training helps and Cara had none. She was defenseless and innocent."

"Yes," Diego muttered. "You have no idea how horrible we felt, how guilty. We never thought for a moment that our beautiful daughter would be grabbed off a sidewalk two blocks from our home, drugged, and driven over the border, and then find herself about to be sold to some *pervertido* overseas."

Tyler watched as he took the pan from the gas stove and carefully poured the steaming chocolate into the four bright-red ceramic mugs. "But you have her back now."

"Yes, and things are settling back into what

they were before." He rinsed out the empty pan beneath the faucet. "Ram and Ali brought her through the worst of it. But you performed something equally important, Tyler."

"What was that?" he wondered.

Diego handed him a bowl that had been in the fridge. "You are breathing life back into Cara." He took off the lid, took a tablespoon and handed it to him. "This is thick, homemade whipped cream. Put a scoop into each mug, please?"

"Sure." He frowned, being careful not to make a mess. Diego, who stood at his side watching, gave him a nod of approval. He licked the spoon afterward, grinning toward Diego.

"You are a man after my own heart," Diego pronounced, clapping Tyler on the back.

As Tyler rinsed off the spoon and his hands, Diego moved a bit closer, lowering his voice.

"My daughter Cara has spoken to us about you. She said that you hold a special place in her heart. Has she told you that?"

Hesitating, Tyler pulled the towel off the hook near the sink, drying his hands. "No . . . she didn't."

Diego grimaced. "My daughter is winsome, beautiful, and has had many heartbreaks with boys in her life. I say boys, not men. The boys following her around wanted only one thing: her body. They did not care about her heart, her dreams, or her soul." Diego looked into Tyler's eyes. "I don't know whether it is because of the trauma of what she survived or perhaps, as Mary and I hoped, she is maturing. We had hoped that she would fall in love with a man someday, not a boy." He scowled, his voice lower so he could not be overheard. "Three days ago, when you and Cara were driving around and you were getting her used to being out and about?"

"Yes?"

"Colin showed up at our door."

Tyler frowned. "Her old boyfriend who abandoned her after she'd been kidnapped?"

"The same," Diego muttered darkly. "He said he'd heard Cara was teaching again. Now, this boy did not ask how Cara was, nor did he explain why he dropped her when he found out she'd been kidnapped. Or," he growled, "if she was even interested in seeing him again. None of those things! I told him that whatever had been between them was gone. I ordered him to leave and never come back to our home or to think that Cara was available to him. Because she wasn't. Not to him. Not EVER."

Tyler heard the grinding rage in Diego's voice, his dark eyes flashing. "Does Cara know he came over to see her?"

"Not yet. Mary and I will talk with her sometime tomorrow. I'm sure our daughter has no interest in a weak, spineless boy like him. She has eyes for another. A real man."

"Oh?" Tyler said, surprised.

Diego poked his chest with his index finger. "Yes. You!"

CHAPTER 7

C ARA COULD HARDLY wait to sit down next
to Tyler on the couch. Christmas morning
meant rich Mexican coffee, a hearty breakfast,
and then everyone gathering in the living room in
front of the tree, where her parents would hand
out the gifts. They'd had delicious coffee, *huevos
rancheros,* and now they were ready for the
distribution of the gifts. This year, there was a gift
from Ali and Ram beneath the tree, too. They
promised that next year, they would be home for
Christmas.

At least she had Tyler with her. He was
dressed in a cream, long-sleeved polo shirt, the
sleeves pushed up to just below his elbows. His
masculinity was always center stage, although he
never seemed to realize or take advantage of it.

He was the polar opposite of Colin, who

strutted around as if being male was a badge of honor, always bragging about what he'd done to make himself stand out and attract women. She was now appreciating men who were comfortable in their skin and with themselves, such as Ram and Tyler—so different from braggarts like Colin.

Cara was given five gifts, and the last one was a small box with a bright gold ribbon wrapped around it. As she took it from her father, she saw on the tag that it was from Tyler. She turned, smiling over at him. "What did you get me?"

He laughed. "Like I'm going to tell you. Remember, I'm black ops?"

She moved her hands around the small, silver foil-wrapped box. "No hints?" She gave him her best pleading look, watching his face grow tender.

"No. A surprise is a surprise. I hope you like it."

"I'm well past surprises, believe me," she quipped, referring to her kidnapping. She saw him give her a sympathetic look as Diego brought over his third gift.

"This is a good surprise," he promised her.

Diego carried a huge package over to Tyler. "Hey I didn't expect anything," he told him shyly.

"You should know better," Diego said with a grin. "And I see you've given each of us a gift, and you didn't have to do that, either."

"You should know better than that," Tyler shot back, laughing with Diego.

Mary sat down in her chair and Diego took his seat, facing the couch where they sat. "I think it's time we open our gifts!" he said to everyone.

Cara knew it would be no surprise that she had knitted her mother and father a gift. Knitting had kept her sane through the worst of her trauma as she sat in her bedroom, rocking in the rocking chair because it, too, soothed her anxiety.

For the next few minutes, she watched her parents open her gifts to them, delight shining on their faces. Her mother's favorite color was red. No surprise there. Her mama was a fiery, passionate personality, just like Ali. Mary loved the red cape that Cara had knitted for her. It would keep her warm during the winter months in the Sonoran Desert. Her father was very pleased to see another long-sleeved, dark-brown cable-knit sweater he could wear in the winter while working in the pecan orchard.

"Aren't you going to open yours?" Tyler suggested to Cara.

"You haven't opened any of yours, *Señor Hutton*."

Chuckling, he said, "Okay, I want to open the biggest one and that's from you."

Cara held her breath, hoping that he would like the gift. As he pulled the dark, navy-blue sweater out of the box, she saw him smile. "Do you like it?"

"It's perfect," he said, holding it up, placing it

against his torso, making sure it fit and the sleeves were long enough. "I like that it's simple and one color. In my line of work, we can't wear bright colors or stand out in any way. We have to blend in." He folded the sweater, placing it in his lap. "Thank you, Cara. You didn't have to do this for me, but I'm glad you did."

She wanted to reach out and touch his cheek as she had in the classroom, but something stopped her. Ever since she'd hugged him, it felt as if he was retreating from her. Now she realized it had been the wrong thing to do. "I watched what you wore when you first got here. Your clothes were all dark, conservative, single colors. I didn't know you couldn't wear brighter colors, but that makes sense to me now."

"Is this machine washable and dryer safe?"

"Sure is," she said, drowning in his blue gaze, wanting desperately to kiss him just once. But this wasn't the time or place. *If ever.* Picking up the small package, she daintily unknotted the bow and slipped the ribbon away from it. Feeling Tyler's gaze on her, she concentrated on removing the silver foil wrapping from around it. She could feel tension rising in him and didn't know why. Maybe he was worried she wouldn't like his gift? Giving him a nervous smile, she said, "I just never expected a gift from you."

"I wanted to give you something that would make you feel good about yourself."

"Hmmm," she teased, placing the wrapping aside, "that sounds mysterious. Now you've made me curious." She pried open the blue velvet jewelry box. Her eyes widened as she peered down at the small brooch and a gasp broke from her lips. Then, she turned her head and met his gaze.

"Tyler! This is beautiful," she sighed, stroking the jewelry, awed by the pin's delicate beauty.

"You like it?"

"Of course! I love butterflies! How did you know?"

"You have a bunch of them up on the wall of your bedroom."

She gave him a sour look. "Your black-ops side again noting little details."

Giving her a nervous smile, he nodded. "Yeah, I guess so." He leaned closer to her, pointing to the gold butterfly that had two filigree wings. "My dad is not only a gem miner, he's also a gemologist and jeweler. He makes my mother gifts like this. These aren't cut glass faceted in the wings of the butterfly, Cara. They are pink, blue, yellow, and green sapphires that he found in the earth, from his mine."

She gasped. "No! Are you serious?" She gulped, realizing this was not a piece of cosmetic jewelry.

"That's eighteen-karat gold from Alaska. For years, my dad was a gold miner before settling down and marrying my mother. He struck it pretty rich up in the Klondike area. He had the gold he panned melted into bars. In the winter, he makes molds and then melts the gold and pours it into them, finishing them off with gemstones he's found at his mine and then sets them into the jewelry."

She stared at the fine, detailed butterfly. It was about the size of quarter with a pin in the back and a gold bail at the top of it for a necklace if she preferred. "Oh, dear ... I thought ... well, this has to be very expensive, Tyler." She gave him a helpless look.

"I called my dad two weeks ago. I remembered he'd created this brooch a few years ago. He liked it so much that he didn't want to sell it, because all his jewelry goes faster than he can create it. He held on to it. The last time I was home from deployment, he gave it to me. He said this was a special piece and felt I should have it."

"What a wonderful story behind this amazing piece," she said, gently touching the shining, glittering stones. There must have been thirty small, faceted sapphires of different colors in the piece. "But why give it to me, Tyler? Didn't your dad give it to you for a special occasion or something?"

He smiled. "Maybe later, when we're alone I'll tell you the rest of the story."

"I love stories."

"I know you do. Your kids love when you read from a book to them because you make the characters come so alive."

Feeling heat rising in her cheeks, she picked up the box and stood. Taking the butterfly out of the box, she said, "Would you pin this on my collar?"

Mary and Diego came over to look at the brooch. They praised it, too. Diego beamed at Tyler.

"That is a priceless gift," Mary said to both of them.

"His father made it," Cara explained.

"It glints the colors of the rainbow," Mary said, nodding, giving Tyler a pleased look.

"I think it is one of my dad's favorite pieces," Tyler told them, taking the brooch from Cara's fingers and carefully pinning it on the lapel of her soft, white angora sweater. "What do you think, Cara?"

"I'm going to go look in the mirror," she said, smiling, touching it.

Tyler watched her turn away and walk down the hall to the bathroom.

Diego clapped Tyler on the shoulder. "We approve, *mi amigo*! Cara will adore that until her last breath. She has no expensive jewelry, so you will always be special to her."

Cara came back, a smile wreathing her lips. "This is incredibly beautiful, Tyler! Please, thank your dad for me? I will treasure this for the rest of my life! I would love to write him a letter and tell him how much I love his work and artistry."

Diego and Mary smiled at one another, retreated to their chairs, and sat down.

"Thank you," Cara whispered, drowning in the blue of Tyler's eyes. She touched the brooch once more. "Promise me you will tell me about this butterfly?"

He remained serious. "Yes, I promise."

December 26

CARA FOUND TYLER out in the garage at ten a.m. He was cleaning up an area where her father had been doing some sanding work on a piece of furniture. Her heart warmed as she watched him sweeping and using a dustpan to carry the curled wood chips to the garbage can kept in one corner. He looked up and smiled.

"What are you doing out here? I thought you were going to go over your lesson plans for January?"

She hungrily absorbed him in a pair of well-worn jeans and a black t-shirt that showed off his powerful physique. Tyler wasn't heavily muscled, reminding her more of a tight spring that when jolted into action made him a lethal bodyguard. "Oh, I was taking a break from it. I was just wondering where you had gone. Mama's in the kitchen whipping up some apple pies and Papa took off for the pecan farm. They had an emergency out there. One of the main water pipes blew and they asked him to come in to oversee the repair of it."

"Your dad shouldn't have to be doing that the day after Christmas," Tyler muttered. "He works out there ten hours a day, five days a week. They could call a pump company and have them do it without demanding that he be there, too." He clipped the broom handle back on the sidewall and placed the dustpan next to it. Rubbing his hands down his jeans, he walked toward the stool where Cara sat, she had pulled one out for him as well. He was pleased to see that she was wearing the butterfly brooch on her dark-blue knit sweater, which, of course, she had made.

"Papa is always afraid of being fired," she confided. "That's why he comes when they tell him to do it. He isn't paid for the extra time he spends there, either. It's wrong. They think they can take advantage of Hispanic people, just as they have for nearly a century in the fields of the US."

He pulled the second stool closer to Cara, sitting down and facing her, about four feet between them. "It isn't fair and never has been." He saw the turbulence in her eyes. They always turned a darker brown when she was upset about something. And when she was happy they were a cinnamon-gold color. "So? What's up? You look like you've got something to say."

"Am I that obvious, Tyler? Really?" she sighed, shaking her head. "I guess I can't hide anything from you."

"We're taught to read people as a matter of course. It just makes you look that much more beautiful to me. There's everything right about showing how you are feeling, Cara. Don't ever lose that part of you, because people can trust you. What they see is what they get."

She pushed the light-blue wool fabric of her trousers down across her thighs, a nervous gesture on her part. "Yesterday, after you gave me this incredible gift," she said, touching the butterfly, "you said we could talk more about why your dad had given it to you."

Now it was his turn to frown. "Oh." The word came out flat, but there were a lot of feelings hidden behind it. He raised his eyes to hers. "I did say that, didn't I?"

"Yes."

"I was married at one time to a lady named Lisa when I was twenty," he began in a low tone. "Looking back on it I wasn't ready to be married or knew what being married meant. I was cocky, full of myself, a risk taker, and thought I was impervious to combat and what it took out of you over time. If I had it to do all over again, I wouldn't have married her." He slowly moved his palms down his thighs. "As it was, my PTSD accumulated over the years. I couldn't communicate with her when I'd come off a deployment. We got into a lot of verbal fights and they were all my fault, not hers. She was trying to get me to open up, to understand my pain, but I just couldn't do it. I didn't know how, but that's not an excuse. She sent me divorce papers when I was twenty-six and over in Afghanistan. I signed them." His hands came to rest and he looked away, unable to stand the sympathy in Cara's eyes. "I truly loved her and I knew this disaster was all on me. I signed the papers because she deserved to be free of me. She deserved happiness . . ."

"I'm so sorry, Tyler. Both of you were in great pain with one another. Ali has talked to me enough about her PTSD and how it has harmed the relationships she's had off and on through the years. She refused to date military guys, just civilians, but she said those men didn't have a clue who she was, the pressures on her, or understand the dangerous world she worked within. It wasn't a fit and it didn't work for her until she and Ram finally settled the bad blood between them." She tilted her head, searching his sad gaze. "Do you think a civilian can marry a military person and make it work?"

"I do, but as I learned with Lisa, it takes a helluva lot of work, of constant inter-communications. I wouldn't open up and she wasn't a mind reader. The two never mixed, like oil and water."

"So it's about the man not speaking up? Letting his wife know how he really feels?"

"Yeah, something like that. But another part of it, Cara, is that no civilian can possibly understand what has happened to us in the military and especially not in combat situations. Not one of them can imagine it, even though they try. If I did this all over again, with hindsight being twenty-twenty, I would have put off marriage until after I left the SEALs. So many SEAL marriages got destroyed. It's a sad situation. Poor Lisa was just another casualty."

"But so were you," she said softly.

"I think Life 101 teaches us things that should be pretty common sense, but that only happens after you're ready to climb out of your twenties and get into your thirties. By that time, you've made a lot of mistakes and learned a lot more—and you can make far more mature decisions."

"Ali and Ram are both near thirty."

"Yes, and I think the way they see each other now has changed their minds from what they thought of each other before. I think that relationship is going to continue to grow into something solid down the line. At least, I hope it does, because they're both good people."

Opening her hands, she asked, "When you gifted me with this butterfly that your father had made, you said there was a story behind it?"

His mouth tightening, he began, "I was a year out of my divorce from Lisa and came home to my parents' place in Montana after deployment because I had no home to come back to stateside. I was pretty depressed. My parents were married in their late twenties and are still in love to this day.

Seeing them still so happy, I broke down and asked my dad what I did wrong in losing the marriage and Lisa. He smiled and went over to one of his cabinets where he kept the best jewelry he'd made. Telling me to hold out my hand, he placed that butterfly brooch in my palm. I sat there feeling so damned defeated. I've excelled at everything I've ever done, Cara. I'd always been a winner. But the divorce found me unprepared. I had no training, no experience of how to deal with the emotions that were continually boiling up in me, and I felt like a loser."

Tyler shifted uncomfortably in the chair. "I asked Dad what he was doing because I knew how much he prized that piece of jewelry. He said that when you love a woman she is your best friend, your lover, and the mother of your children. He tapped the butterfly and told me that a woman is like a butterfly. You had to respect her, treat her as an equal, or she would fly away from the man who wanted to control her. Most of all, he told me that while women wanted our physical strength and good looks, what they really wanted was us to give them our hearts."

He shook his head, "I asked him what that meant—I hadn't a clue what he was getting at. He said that you could not bully, manipulate, push, or lie to a woman. That love between two people consisted of equality and mutual respect. A woman was the butterfly of a man's world as he saw and understood it. I knew how much he loved this brooch and I tried to give it back to him, telling him that I got the message, that I didn't need the brooch. He has large hands, Cara, much larger than mine. He cupped my hand, telling me that I should keep this for a woman who was everything to me that he'd shared earlier. I was to give it to her because in time, he said, 'You'll be more mature and you'll understand what I've just shared with you'." Tyler forced himself to look up at Cara, her eyes glistening with a sheen of tears. Her hands were clasped between her breasts where her heart lay.

Just then, his cell phone rang.

MENTALLY CURSING, TYLER answered the

phone. "Hutton," he snapped. Dammit, he'd just unveiled his heart to Cara and now this! It couldn't have been worse timing. Glancing over at her, he saw her sniffling and fighting her tears, her face soft and sculptured by light and dark, her long black hair slightly curled, framing her oval face.

"Tyler, it's Wyatt Lockwood. Sorry to bother you, but we just received news that the Mexican Marines stormed Emilio Azarola's villa—yes, the same people who kidnapped Cara."

Shock bolted through him. "There was an ongoing mission? You knew about this?"

"Sure did, son. It was top secret because our Mexican Marine friends asked that it be so, and we agreed. Captain Gomez of the Marines teamed up with an Artemis op to create a joint, long-term mission to hunt the sick bastard down and capture him. Only, when they stormed the villa, Azarola was killed along with twenty of his men. No one was left alive in that snake pit. The Marines blew up the villa, brought in bulldozers and leveled the area. It was a warning to other drug kingpins in the state of Sonora that the Marines were coming for them, too."

Tyler glanced over to see a sudden worried look on Cara's face. "Can I tell her and her family what happened?"

"Absolutely. They deserve to have closure on this, too. And of course, that means your gig as a

PSD for her is over. There will be a Delos jet at Davis-Monthan at 1000 tomorrow morning to pick you up. I think Cara will like the good news. Ali has been worried that Azarola and his men would drive into Tucson and kidnap her once more. Now, everyone can rest easy. None of Azarola's men are alive. No one is going to kidnap her, so you tell her she's safe now, okay?"

Tyler's throat tightened as he held her gaze. There was tension in her expression, her full lips now thinned. "Yes, I'll let her and her family know."

"Good enough. We all miss you, so we're looking forward to having you back in our department."

Tyler hung up, feeling as if his heart had just fallen out of his body. He knew this day would come, sooner or later, and that was why he'd tried so hard to maintain emotional distance from Cara. He slid the cell phone back into his shirt pocket, meeting her troubled gaze.

"That was Wyatt, from Artemis. He called to tell me to let you and your family know that a Mexican Marines joint task force has just killed Azarola and twenty of his men. They wiped them out." He saw her eyes snap open, shock hitting her.

"Oh," she cried out softly, her hand against her throat. "Really? He's really dead?"

Hearing the relief in her hoarse tone, he gave

a bare nod. "It's over, Cara. You don't have to go to bed at night thinking that he or his men are going to cross the border and come here to kidnap you again." He reached out, covering her other hand that was knotted into a fist in her lap. "It's over, *mi corazón*." He knew enough Spanish to say that endearment to her and he meant every word of it. She was his heart. There was such love that came to her eyes when he gruffly spoke those words to her. She turned her hand, her fingers wrapping around his.

"I-I'm in shock, Tyler . . ."

"But at least this time it's good shock."

"Do Ali and Ram know about this?"

"Yes. Everyone's celebrating back at Artemis. This is a day for the good guys and girls. After the Marines took the villa, they removed the bodies, brought in a bulldozer, and plowed that place into the ground. It's a warning to other drug lords who live in Sonora that the Marines are coming after them, too. It's the start of a huge multi-country task force effort to eradicate all the other Azarolas."

She released his hand and stood up, nervously looking toward the closed door that went to the kitchen from the garage. "Can we tell Mama and Papa?"

"Absolutely," he said, standing. Walking up to her, he gently turned her toward him, his hands resting lightly on her shoulders, drowning in her shining eyes filled with joy. "Today is the first day of the rest of your life, Cara. It's as if this chapter in your life is over. Now," he continued, looking around the quiet, shadowed garage, "you're starting a new one with new possibilities. Like the butterfly I gave you, it's a symbol of freedom. In the chrysalis stage, you were imprisoned by Azarola. Now, you've cracked the chrysalis, unfolded your beautiful wings and can fly free, living your life just the way you want."

He could see the shock and growing relief now that her worst fears were gone. But he was going to be gone, too. *Very shortly.* Not having the stomach to tell her yet, he urged her toward the stairs leading to the kitchen. She flashed him the prettiest smile, her cheeks a bright pink, her steps far more confident than ever before. It was at that moment that Tyler knew he'd fallen in love with her—the deepest, and forever kind.

What the hell had he done? How had it happened? He stuffed his feelings down and focused on Cara's bubbling cry as she opened the door, running toward her parents in the kitchen. As he stood back, he saw Mary burst into tears over the good news, grabbing her slender daughter. Diego wrapped his arms around both of the women. It was humbling to see that a man could cry right along with his wife and daughter, and Tyler had the ultimate respect for men like Diego because they were so rare.

He, too, knew how to cry, but too often he'd stuff it down instead of allowing tears to fall. That was part of his problem. Right now, there was a lump the size of a walnut in his throat and Tyler felt as if he had to forcefully pull in air and then expel it, or he'd suffocate. The sobs in the kitchen were filled with relief, with celebration, and soon, the three of them were laughing and giggling, arms around one another.

"Come!" Diego urged him. "Come celebrate Cara's freedom with us!" he said, making a sharp gesture for Tyler to come and share in the happiness with them.

Tyler grinned shyly, hands in his pockets, slowly walking toward these people he had come to love. He drowned in Cara's eyes as she stepped away, opening her arm, and drawing him beside her. And as she did, Diego's strong, leather-brown arm curved around his back. On the other side was Mary's plump arm gripping her husband and Cara. For a moment, there was silence, but it was a silence of relief, as if the four of them were breathing as one, their hearts pounding in unison. He closed his eyes, feeling the fierce love this family shared between them. How he missed being near his own parents, missing that same palpable love that wound through him like soft rain after a thunderstorm, the drops hitting the parched area of his heart that yearned for exactly this: being wanted, being loved, being held, and being with a loving family.

As Diego patted the center of his back, he guided Tyler's head against all of their bowed heads. He whispered a prayer to the Lady of Guadalupe, Mother Mary, his voice choked, tears rolling unashamedly down his lean, sun-darkened cheeks, his other arm drawing his wife and daughter as close as possible.

Tyler heard Mary speaking in Pascua Yaqui, her voice husky with tears. He didn't know what she said, but whatever it was, it was passionate, fierce, and deeply grateful.

Cara whispered brokenly, heads bowed against one another, "Oh, Lady, thank you for taking care of all of us! We humbly thank you from the bottom of all our hearts for looking over us. Please bless Tyler, who is your warrior guardian caring for all of us . . ."

Her trembling voice broke something so old and so deep within him that it sounded, literally, like glass being shattered. Hot tears were rolling out from beneath his tightly shut lids, his arms around them, holding on to them, feeling their hearts beating wildly with such jubilation that he'd never felt so thankful as at this moment. They had all made him a part of their family and he'd be forever grateful for their open arms, welcoming him into their lives.

Finally, Mary broke them apart, telling them to go to the table, that they would pour a bit of their beloved Madeira wine that they drank only on very, very special occasions, to celebrate the good news. Tyler tried to offer his help, but Mary shook her finger in his face.

"Go! Be with my daughter where you belong! She needs you now more than ever."

The words pulverized him and he turned, feeling a heavy weight settle on his yearning heart. God, he didn't want to tell them right now that he had to leave tomorrow. *Not now.* This family had been through months of unending hell, unrelenting fear and anxiety. He sat down next to Cara, with Diego at one end of the table. Both were glowing with joy.

Mary brought over four small, beautiful hand-cut crystal goblets. She set them down in front of Diego and then handed him the cherished bottle of Madeira. Diego nodded his thanks, opened the bottle, and carefully poured the amber liquid into each one. Mary sat down at his left, across the table from himself and Cara. Both women were still wiping their damp cheeks dry, but their eyes sparkled like stars glimmering in the darkness of the desert night sky.

Diego handed the first glass to his wife, holding her gaze, love clearly being communicated between them. Next, he handed one to his daughter, a catch in his voice as he choked out, "*Mi hermosa hija*, to my beautiful daughter."

Next, he handed one to Tyler. "You have

become like a son to us, *mi amigo*."

More of that old, hard, dark substance within Tyler shattered. He held Diego's glistening eyes, beyond ecstatic that his daughter was no longer the target of a dreaded drug lord.

Diego picked up his glass and held it up. "I toast our Lady of Guadalupe. We thank her for our daughter's life and an end to our family's nightmare."

Tyler took a sip of the sweet aperitif wine, silently agreeing with Diego's low, emotional words.

How was he going to tell them he was leaving? It was no accident Diego called him "a son to us." And out in the garage, he hadn't helped matters at all. He'd called Cara "my heart," and he meant those branding words with his soul. He could tell his roughly spoken endearment wasn't lost on her, either. He'd seen the desire leap to her eyes, the love in them when he'd said it—the feeling was mutual.

He loved Cara, and he knew Diego and Mary loved him and felt they both saw him as a decent man to become Cara's husband. He had grown fond of them. They were good people who worked hard and tried their best. Cara and Ali were a reflection of them, both stellar human beings in his book.

He had to talk with Cara privately, knowing this was a blow she did not see coming. His whole life had taken on a rainbow of happiness just from being around Cara. Her family was perfect. Love was everywhere. *So now, what?*

CHAPTER 8

December 26

C ARA WALKED WITH Tyler to the garage after the family's toast, feeling positively giddy, her step light, a smile hovering around her lips, her eyes shining with hope once again. This was the Cara before the kidnapping, Tyler realized. They sat down at the two stools at the wood-working counter and she gave him a searching look.

"Are you all right, Tyler. You look . . . well . . . worried."

He shrugged. "It depends. Look," he began quietly, holding her gaze, "Wyatt is my boss at Artemis. In that phone call earlier, he said that my mission as a PSD for you was now finished."

Cara stiffened, her eyes widening. "What does that mean?"

Hearing the sudden drop, the terror in her

voice, he winced inwardly. "It means that a Delos jet is going to land at Davis-Monthan at ten a.m. tomorrow morning and fly me back to Virginia." He wasn't going to string Cara along or try to soften the blow. It was like taking off a Band-Aid—better to rip it off quickly than slowly.

"Oh, no . . ." she cried, staring at him. "Why so soon?"

His heart sank. If Tyler ever had any doubts that they shared something good between them, it was proven by her reaction. "They need me, Cara. Everyone at Artemis is a specialist of some sort. When a mission comes up where someone with my skills is needed, if I'm available, I'm the one that goes."

Her hand pressed to her lips. "You have to go on another mission right after you leave us? Where? Will it be dangerous?"

Tyler slid off the stool took the steps to where she sat, placing his hands gently on her shoulders. He could feel the tension in them beneath her sweater. It was the anguish in her voice that tore through him. "I don't know. Wyatt is the head of Mission Planning. He chooses the people he feels will be best suited for something, and it sounded like he needed me right away. He wouldn't have chosen me if I were still your PSD, Cara. I'd have stayed here, guarding you instead. But with Azarola out of the picture, you're safe now."

"I see . . . yes, you're right," she agreed, placing her hand on his chest.

He smoothed the sweater along her shoulders, wanting desperately to hold her, kiss her, and love the hell out of her until she fainted with pleasure. "I'll be fine, Cara. Most missions aren't dangerous, so I don't want you to worry. Okay?"

Where there had been such joy in them seconds ago, her sable eyes with gold dappling had turned dark brown, telling him just how much the news was affecting her. She was now fighting back tears, trying to be brave.

He felt her hand like a hot brand rest on his shirt, and he wanted desperately for her to continue to explore him as a man who loved her. But he felt caught in a messy, confusing net of circumstances. "You have your life back now, Cara. You can be like that butterfly pin I gave you. You're free . . ." he rasped.

"But I don't want you to go! I know you must, but my heart feels torn in half." She slipped off the stool with his hands still on her shoulders and moved closer to him, placing her hands on his chest, looking earnestly up into his stormy gaze. "You made me want to live again, Tyler. You moved me out of the past and back into the present. I dream now because of you." She swallowed, and then boldly added, "I've dreamed of us together. Forever."

"What?" he managed hoarsely. "Do you really mean that, Cara?"

She whispered unsteadily, "I've dreamed of us being together ever since I met you, Tyler. Now I can tell you because you're leaving, but I couldn't say anything earlier about how I felt because you were here to guard me, not to begin a relationship. So often, I would have moments when I would feel you wanting to tell me something—and you couldn't. You don't know how many times I wanted to touch you like this, to talk with you on a personal, intimate level. I thought it was all in my head, Tyler. I couldn't trust myself because of my symptoms but the more you were with me, the more I realized that what I felt toward you was very, very real. It wasn't my overactive imagination."

He stared at her, the softness of her palms against his chest making his skin tighten. His heart was pounding so hard he could barely hear her.

"I've wanted you just as much, but I couldn't go there, Cara. What you felt from me is real." He caressed her shoulders, seeing hope flare in her eyes. "But we need time to feel our way through everything that's happened to us. I was drawn to you when Wyatt handed me your photo to discuss the PSD. I thought it was just me. I honestly didn't come here looking to be drawn to you and I'm sure it was the last thing on your mind, too."

She reached up, caressing his stubbly cheek.
"You may be right, but somewhere along the line,
I began to feel differently toward you, Tyler. You
have no idea how tough it was not to ask you a
hundred personal questions. I wanted to know so
much about you, the person, but I was afraid to
ask because you'd made it clear from the beginning you were strictly here to protect me."

He caught her hand, kissing the back of it
and then placing it against his heart. But what
could he bring to her? He'd already hurt Lisa. He
never wanted to hurt Cara like that. And yet, her
luminous eyes were shining with love as she held
his gaze, melting his heart with his desperate need
for her. She made him want things he hadn't
thought he could ever have again.

"You inspire me to dream again, Cara," he
began roughly, moving his hand back and forth
across hers. "I've been afraid to dream because
when I married Lisa, I wanted it all: I wanted her,
I wanted to see her pregnant with our child, I
wanted to be with her when she gave birth, and I
wanted to have a family."

Cara could see that the man she loved was at
war with himself. His sensitive, beautiful mouth
was tight, his eyes shining with tears.

"All I wanted was a family, like the loving
one I'd come from. I wanted that for us and our
unborn children. I thought it would be easy to
have one, but the whole relationship became a

nightmare instead."

She stepped forward, resting her brow against his upper chest, closing her eyes, and hearing the hard beating of his heart. As his arm came around her waist, holding her close, she felt him nestle his head beside her own. How long did they stand that way? It seemed forever.

"Sometimes," she began softly, "the first step is the hardest one to take, Tyler. I learned that when I came home after captivity. Ali, Ram, and my family helped me with that first one. But it was you who helped me take that second, third, and fourth step toward getting better." She lifted her head away just enough to drown in his turbulent blue eyes. He was so close . . . close enough to kiss. Pushing up on her toes, she brushed the tortured line of his mouth, her kiss slow, filled with invitation and warmth.

A jolt of fire plunged through Tyler as her soft lips touched and then coaxed his to relax. Her breath was moist, a few strands of her black hair tickling his chin. The scent of honey surrounded him, his nostrils flaring, drinking in her womanly fragrance. Never had he expected her to be so bold and kiss him! It took exactly four heartbeats for him to shake off his shock and accept her invitation. He had no right to kiss her. *None at all.* What could he offer her? *Nothing.* He didn't think he could offer Cara what she truly deserved.

Yet, her lips pillowed against his, shy but hungry, and he tasted her for the first time. The Madeira wine was sweet upon them, and he groaned as she pressed her hips against his, letting him know just what was at stake between them. Yes, she was committed to him, and wanted a serious relationship.

His mind liquefied and he couldn't think coherently. All he could do was feel his lower body explode with raw animal need of this tender, beautiful, trusting woman. Her mouth opened and he took her more surely, reining in his primal desire to consume her in every possible way. Knowing how to love a woman and make her soar beneath him, he ached to do that right now with Cara. He was getting lost in the texture and shape of her mouth, feeling her smile against his. Yes, this was right, and his erection was powerful as his body recognized the truth of their connection. He knew that Cara would feel it straining against his jeans, no matter how he tried to hide it.

He glided against her lips, opening them, tasting her more deeply, and allowing her to let him know just how far she wanted him to go. When her tongue shyly touched his, he growled, that old, familiar sexual hunger rising swiftly, nearly overtaking his need to be slow and responsive to Cara. She wasn't a neophyte. She knew what she wanted—and she knew what *he* wanted.

Unwillingly, Tyler pulled away from her lips, tasting Cara, never wanting to forget this moment with her. As he opened his eyes, he saw her long, black lashes lying against her golden skin, her cheeks rosy, flushed with excitement—with need. As her lashes lifted, he saw her cinnamon-colored eyes dappled with gold in their depths. He was mesmerized by her beauty, the silence winding around them, embracing them as they stood in one another's arms.

"I know you have to go, *mi amado*. My beloved." She touched his cheek, holding his gaze. "We will find a way, even though there will be so much distance between us. I don't want you leaving without knowing that you hold my heart in your hands, Tyler. I have never been attracted to a man as I am to you. This is real. It's wonderful and it's frightening because I don't know what's going to happen when you leave us tomorrow."

"You're the bravest person I've ever met," he managed, his voice strangled sounding. "You're not afraid to step into a relationship with me, Cara, and that blows my mind."

She managed a small smile. "Why would I be afraid?"

"My past," he said heavily, moving his fingers through her silky hair. "I'm not a good bet, Cara. I've already proven that by losing Lisa and my marriage. He peered intently down at her. "And you're *still* willing to risk your heart with me knowing that? I'm not in a safe job. I know how much you worry, sweetheart." He moved his hand across her hair, his gaze coming back to hers. "This is serious, Cara."

"No one lives on an island," she whispered, pushing a few strands of his dark hair off his furrowed brow. "You've learned from your past, Tyler. We all have. I trust you, and I'm not afraid to let you hold my heart."

He groaned and eased her away from him just a few inches. "I don't lead a normal life, Cara. I never know when I'll be home or somewhere overseas. You're the kind of woman who, when she gives a man her heart, does it forever."

"Do you want it to work?" she demanded pertly, giving him a searching look.

He liked this strong, feminine side of Cara. She wasn't afraid to do a full frontal, calling him out. Making him responsible for what he said and testing if he really meant it. "I'd like nothing more in this world than for it to work out between us, Cara." He slid his hands slowly up and down her upper arms, watching that fiery glint come to her eyes. He wondered just how much of Cara he had yet to meet, once hidden by her trauma. She was hardly a wilting lily in this heated moment between them. She knew what she wanted: him.

His ego gloried in her bold desire for him and her willingness to come forward and claim him as her own. But the wounded part of him shrank in terror of being hurt once more. Had his job situation changed enough? He no longer had anxiety, allowing him to be open once more. Could he give marriage a hundred percent this time? The desire to teach her so much about her lovely body and gift her with his experience flowed powerfully through him. It was a part of love, a *wonderful* part. How badly he wanted to cave in to Cara's pleading words and her logic.

"Then," she said throatily, "let's stay in touch after you leave, okay? I'm not giving up on you, Tyler. And don't you dare give up on me!"

Managing a shadow of a grin, he slid his fingers through her hair. "I *want* to stay in touch with you." *Forever.* But he couldn't voice the words, as much as he wanted to. Seeing her expression lighten, filling with hope, and her innocent trust filling him as well, he rasped, "I don't know where this will go, Cara."

"I do, and I want us to have the courage to find out. Together."

They both realized that their original situation had changed one-hundred-eighty degrees. Now, he was the wounded one, the person who lacked courage to try because his fear was holding him back.

"Then continue to be courageous for both of

us," he coaxed, tenderly grazing her cheek. "I know many things about us would have to meet your expectations, and I don't want to disappoint you."

Fondly, he looked around the garage. "This is your home. You were born here and you want to stay close to your parents here in Tucson. That will never change, and your love of your kindergarten children fills your heart with a joy that few people ever experience. I wouldn't want to take any of that away from you. These things are a part of your foundation, who you are. They can't be moved away from, minimized, traded, or told to go away."

Her eyes sparkled, an impish glint in them. She tapped his chest smartly. "Then, Mr. Hutton, you'd better think outside the box and figure something out. Come home to me, *mi amado*. I will be waiting here for as long as I draw a breath on this earth—waiting for you. You cannot allow fear to keep your heart hidden from me anymore."

February 14
EVERY FIBER WITHIN Tyler was screaming for him to hurry up, to press down on the accelerator of the rental car he was driving on I-10 west. In the seat next to him was a huge bouquet of pink

roses and a second one of red roses. Beside the bouquets were two large, heart-shaped boxes of the best Belgian chocolates he could find when he'd finished his assignment there. In his pocket was a bright-red velvet box with a set of wedding rings, created and designed by his father, for Cara.

She and her family knew none of this was speeding towards her.

As he drove through the dusk, the sky opened up with horizontal stripes of pink, gold, and red, great colors for this special, loving day. His heart was bursting with unexpected news that he knew would rock Cara's world and his own. How badly he wanted to see her! Just that one precious kiss had fed him in ways he'd never realized until he left on a European assignment to Brussels. It was nearly five p.m. and the winter sky was beautiful in the Sonoran Desert—a helluva lot better than the ice, snow, and cold of Europe and the rest of America. Living out here had its undeniable perks.

Cara knew he was coming to see her. He wouldn't just drop back into her life after being gone for nearly two months without some kind of warning. His hands opened and closed around the steering wheel as he tried to tamp down his own excitement at seeing her in person once more. As soon as he'd arrived in Alexandria, Virginia, Ram and Ali had picked him up and whisked off to Artemis for a late evening mission meeting. There, Wyatt Lockwood and his team had laid out his new assignment: helping the Belgian government hunt down and find terrorists. He spoke enough French, the language most often used in that part of Belgium, and could eavesdrop on conversations. He would be working with Belgian officials as they tried to destroy terrorist cells they knew were hiding in Brussels. They needed a combat medic to accompany their teams as they explored these areas. With the types of weapons that the terrorists used, victims would bleed out before they could reach a hospital.

Artemis provided topnotch combat medics, placing one in each of the teams. It was a good idea, which Tyler endorsed. Luckily, in the six-week mission, his team had no casualties. Cara and her family could know nothing of the mission.

Now, the mission was over. What would Cara think about his news? It was life changing, and he knew Mary and Diego would be shocked. For once, it was good news, and he was the messenger being sent by Artemis to give it to them.

Tonight should be a happy night for all of them. The only fly in the ointment was Cara's possible reaction to his proposal of marriage. In rare Skype calls to one another, neither of them had referred to their having fallen in love with one another. Tonight he planned to do exactly that. But he would have to get Cara alone to find out what she wanted with this long-distance relationship of theirs. *Would she say yes?*

Leaving the freeway, he drove down another avenue going south. In a few minutes, he would arrive at the Montero home. Missing Cara so much, he'd come to realize in their separation that she fulfilled him in ways that Lisa never had. The women had very different personalities, and Cara fed his soul, while Lisa had warmed his heart. Cara was everything he'd dreamed of having. But he could lose her if he didn't begin sharing his true feelings with her. He was still a work-in-progress on that front!

But now he was determined to do it. The drive to settle down, to have a family, had become a compulsion. Maybe it was his age and maturity, or wanting this dream he'd had as a kid actually come true. He'd find out in a few minutes.

In the glow of the brilliant red, pink, and gold sunset, Tyler saw all three members of the Montero family standing out on the porch, waiting impatiently for him to arrive. He grinned, feeling a lot of his tension dissolving. As he turned into the garage area, the flash of head-lights showed Mary in a bright-red skirt that fell to her ankles and her favorite white, long-sleeved blouse with ruffles at the throat. Diego was dressed as usual in a pair of clean jeans, a chambray shirt, sleeves rolled up to his elbows, and wearing the same pair of beat-up cowboy boots.

Cara stood out, wearing a soft, clingy pink dress with a v-shaped neck to show off her slenderness. The dress fell to her knees and she was wearing white sandals on her feet. Her black hair was drawn up on her head, several silver combs keeping it in place. She looked so excited—but so was he.

Turning off the engine, he climbed out. He'd worn a dark-blue sports coat over a white shirt, with tan chinos. Tyler had thought about wearing a tie, too, but he knew the Monteros were a laid-back family who didn't judge people on what they did or did not wear. So he'd left the tie on the front seat beneath the gifts he'd brought.

Waving to them, he walked around the car, opened the passenger-side door, and gathered up everything. He'd gotten two bouquets: one for Mary and the other for Cara. Balancing everything, he pushed the door shut with the toe of his shoe.

"Tyler!"

Cara came running around the end of the car, her smile welcoming and huge.

"Hey," he called, smiling at her as he halted. He saw she had pinned the butterfly brooch on the left side of her dress. That was reassuring!

She laughed as she halted, eyeing his arms full of flowers and boxes of candy. "You came prepared for Valentine's Day, didn't you?"

He nodded. "Flowers and candy for you and your mom. I figured I'd give Diego the chocolates." He saw her expression grow tender as she came forward, placing her hand on his upper arm. She leaned forward, brushing his recently shaven cheek with a kiss.

"All I want," she whispered, "is to be with you sometime tonight when we can talk." She straightened. "Mama and Papa can hardly wait to see you. Mama made a Valentine's Day cake and Papa has the vanilla ice cream ready for it. I hope you're a little hungry?" she asked, slipping her arm into his.

Tyler wasn't going to settle for a quick peck on the cheek. As she came beside him, he leaned over, capturing her smiling lips.

They halted near the car, the flowers squeezed between them as he hungrily kissed her. Even better, Cara's lips were just as warm and sweet as he remembered. As they eased apart, he said, "Let's make a date to meet in the garage later. Okay?"

"Okay," she said breathlessly, walking with him around the car and heading for the porch where her parents stood waiting for them.

Mary was stunned by his gift of red roses, all

two dozen of them. He knew in Mexico and other Latin countries that a kiss on each cheek was welcomed. This time, Mary kissed him a third time, a sign that he was more than just a friend, and it made him feel wanted. He moved to Diego and shook the man's strong, sunburned hand.

"Are you giving me the chocolates?" he teased, taking them with a nod of thanks.

"I didn't think you'd want to eat the flowers," Tyler joked, grinning.

Diego laughed deeply. "*Sí*, you are right about that!"

Tyler turned to Cara. "These are for you. I know your favorite color is pink," he said, slipping the two dozen roses wrapped in gold foil with a red ribbon, into her arms.

Cara leaned over, inhaling the roses' rich aroma. She made a humming sound in her throat. "They smell so good, Tyler. Thank you!"

If her parents were as surprised as he was that she came and kissed him full on the mouth, they didn't seem shocked at all. Instead, as Tyler finished the quick kiss, he saw them nod and give one another knowing looks. "How about if I hold on to the chocolates for you until we get inside?"

"As long as you don't start eating them without me," Cara laughed.

Diego opened the door, ushering them into the brightly lit house. He went directly to the kitchen, bringing down two large glass vases. Tyler put the candies on the table.

"You are staying with us, aren't you?" Cara asked.

"Absolutely."

"For how long?"

He saw the concern in her expression. Touching a long, slightly curled strand of her black hair near her temple, he said, "I'll tell you more about that after we sit down at the table, okay?"

"Sure. I'm going to help Mama and Papa serve the cake and ice cream."

"Can I help?"

"You can pour the fresh coffee," she said, pointing to the four yellow mugs sitting next to the percolator.

Tyler liked helping, and the kitchen was large enough for four people to comfortably do their thing. Soon, the pink frosted Valentine's Day cake had been expertly cut and placed on the dessert plates. He helped Mary bring them to the table after taking steaming mugs of coffee to the table earlier.

As they all settled at the table, bowls of vanilla ice cream next to the white cake with pink frosting, Tyler knew it was time.

"I have a lot of news that I want to share with you," he told them. "I hope you're ready for some earthquake surprises."

CHAPTER 9

"I HAVE SOME great news to share with all of you," Tyler began, after they finished their cake and ice cream. Cara sat opposite him with Mary, and Diego sat at the head of the table.

"Tal Culver-Lockwood, is the CEO of Artemis and my boss, Wyatt's, wife. When I flew back to Virginia, I dropped into her office to talk with her." He gave Cara a warm look. "I said that when this mission was completed, I was going to turn in my resignation. She asked me why. I told her I'd met a woman that I wanted to share time and space with, and that I wanted to pursue a serious relationship with her."

Silence reigned in the kitchen. He moved his hands around the mug of coffee. The look in Cara's eyes touched his heart, and fed him hope. There was such love burning in them for him. Yearning to be alone with her, he went on. "Tal wasn't too happy to hear that I would leave Artemis. She asked what I wanted, so that if it was possible, I would stay with Artemis. I told her I needed to live in Tucson so I could continue to explore my relationship with Cara."

Mary sighed, giving her daughter a joyous look. Diego nodded wisely, and Cara was close to tears.

"She surprised me when she said that the Human Resources Department, Mission Planning, and she were in top-secret mode with plans to place satellite offices of Artemis around the world. Artemis has grown so fast, it has become the go-to civilian security company that every US-government security agency hired over a year ago—and countries friendly to America also heavily use our services and connections. All of them wanted Artemis to put smaller offices in major cities around the world. Here, along the border, they are putting an office in El Paso, Texas and one in Tucson and Phoenix. Tal told me that she had just told Ali and Ram that they were going to be transferred to Tucson to manage that office."

All three of the Monteros gasped. Mary burst into tears as Diego held her. Cara placed her hands against her lips, staring in shock across the table at him.

"Ali and Ram were told about this an hour before I flew out here. Tal wanted me to break the news to you as a family because I'll be among the employees stationed here, as well. I'm sure, probably within the next half hour or so, Ali and Ram will be calling you to share the details of the good news with all of you."

"Oh," Mary cried, "this is such wonderful news, Tyler!" She wept loudly while Diego gently patted her heaving shoulders.

Tyler looked over at Cara. "It's official. The Building Department at Artemis has had plans for this office for a while. They have been constructing the office on Speedway, near the Arizona State University. In another month, we'll be moving into it."

Cara shook her head. "This—this is so unexpected but wonderful. Are you all right with it, Tyler?"

"I'm delighted, to say the least," he assured her, his voice low and heavy with emotion. "How about you, Cara? Can you stand me underfoot all the time?"

She laughed a little, giddy childlike laugh as she wiped tears from her eyes. "I can hardly speak—of course I can!"

"I thought maybe tomorrow you could help me find a home to buy. Maybe nearby, near your school and parents." Because he honored the tight bonds of love that held this family through good and bad times, he understood they would prefer having Cara nearby. Part of the reason

Cara had been able to overcome her kidnapping was because of the love and support they'd given her.

She smiled coyly. "I have a surprise for you, too, Tyler. There was a beautiful cream-colored adobe home just a half-mile away from here. After you left, I looked at it and bought it. I knew it was time that I get my own place, but I still wanted to be close to my parents. It sits out in the desert, and there's a two-mile dirt road that leads you to the home. It's quiet and away from city sounds and lights. I'd like to show it to you after Ali and Ram's phone call."

He saw the look in her eyes, that glint of challenge and desire. "I'd like that," he said, pleasantly surprised. In the two months that he had been gone, Cara had continued her healing and he could see her newfound confidence radiating from her. How she inspired him with her quiet inner strength!

"Good. I'll tell you more about it on the porch swing tonight," she said, giving him a happy smile. Cara stood and retrieved a box of tissues from one end of the kitchen counter. Halting at the table, she pulled several tissues and placed them in her mother's hand.

"When are they going to call?" Diego asked Tyler.

He looked at his watch. "Probably in about fifteen minutes or so."

"This is all so incredible!" Cara said, giving her father a huge grin. "We'll all be together, just like we always wanted. And they'll have to buy a house, too! I'm sure they'll want something close to you, Mama and Papa."

"I'm sure they will," Tyler said, "and best of all, Ali and Ram have both been removed from the mission roster. They will no longer undertake ops. Rather, they want to work for Artemis in-house, providing consultation support, and they can do that through Skype and teleconferences."

"That's even better news," Diego said, joy in his voice. "We worry so much about both of them when they go out in the field."

"Y-yes," Mary whispered brokenly, blotting her eyes, "I want my daughters safe. I want you and Ram safe, as well."

"Well," Tyler said to her, "I've canceled my mission readiness status, too. It's official that I'll never go out on another mission again. I'll be an in-house specialist, just like Ali and Ram, here in Tucson."

Mary sighed and nodded happily, looking relieved. Diego gave Tyler a pleased look, and Cara stood up.

"Shall we go sit out on the porch swing, Tyler? It's a warm evening," she invited, holding out her hand to him as she came around the end of the table.

Tyler rose, excusing himself. He knew Ali

would be calling shortly and was sure there would be a long discussion between her, Ram, and the Montero family. "Sounds good," he agreed, sliding his hand into hers.

CARA TRIED TO settle her fluttery stomach. It was nerves, she was sure. She sat down in the center of the swing and Tyler came and sat next to her, sliding his arms around her shoulders. He drew her near and she rested her head against his shoulder, closing her eyes. "I feel as if this is all a dream," she admitted in a wispy voice.

Tyler pushed the swing gently with his toe, looking up into the dark sky, the stars a glittering coverlet. "Me too." He leaned over, kissing her soft, silky hair. "You never told me you moved out of here and bought a house."

"I wanted to make sure that I could live alone, first. After you left, I wasn't sure I would be strong enough, but I had to try—and it worked. I'm happy having my own home. It's been good for me, Tyler."

"You've been coming out of a long tunnel of captivity, Cara. It takes time. Still, that was a huge step to take, especially since you had always lived at home."

"It was time I grew up, then," she said, lifting her head and looking up into Tyler's deeply-shadowed face. The light from the living room window accentuated his high cheekbones and strong chin.

"We're always growing," he agreed. "That was a brave step you took. Do you like your new home?"

She smiled a little. "It's a rather large place, six acres surrounding it, but at night, when it's not too cold, I open a window so I can hear the coyotes howling in the distance. I love the sounds of nature instead of hearing cars passing by my parents' home."

He looked down at her and the silence grew between them. "The time apart from you was a special hell for me. I missed seeing you every day, Cara. Missed whatever you thought about all the things we talked about. God, I was lonely." He caressed her cheek, holding her luminous gaze. "I don't know when I fell in love with you, but I have. Maybe it began when I saw your photo when we were mounting the mission to extract you and those German women from the villa. After we got you out of that hellhole, I was pretty busy trying to help the other ladies, but I first saw your strength that night. You weren't crying like the other women. There was something special about you, although at that moment, I wasn't sure we were going to get you all out of there alive. Things were dicey right up until we got you loaded into that Black Hawk."

She felt his fingers lightly touch her cheek. "I remember seeing you, but it was so dark and we were all so scared, Tyler. It was only after you and the other men flew with us in the helicopter that you made such a powerful impression on me. You were so kind and patient with us women. Later, at the Marine base where we landed, I got to see you in the hospital emergency room where we were all taken. It was your voice, your gentleness, that soothed us all. You knew a little German, and you had a way of communicating that helped us all so much."

He slid his hand into hers. "I knew you were scared out of your mind because Ali and Ram were still back there in the mountains, acting as a rear guard so we could escape. The drug soldiers were hunting them from the villa but we never told any of you that. God knows, you'd been through enough."

"Yes, but later after I had been seen by a doctor, you came in and talked to me. You told me not to worry after I kept pressing you for answers about my sister, promising me that Ali and Ram would get out of there in one piece. I believed you," she said, lifting her lashes, drowning in his shadowed gaze. "Tonight, after I get to talk with Ali and Ram . . ."

"Yes?"

"I want you to come home with me, Tyler." She saw the heat and yearning in his eyes, and tightening her hand around his, she sat up, facing him. "I love you. And I've known for some time that we were falling in love with one another. I don't know how it happened, either, but it did. I can hardly believe that you're here, and that you're going to stay here from now on."

"I want to build a life with you, Cara. We need time to slow down and start living together like real people." He saw her smile a little and nod. "I don't know where this is going or where it will end up. I know what I hope happens and will put my heart and soul into it to make it a dream come true for both of us."

"How would you feel if you moved in and lived with me, Tyler? To really find out what we have? Put it to a test?"

He sat there digesting her gentle suggestion, seeing the hope in her eyes, her slender fingers feeling warm and good around his. "What about your parents? What will they think of us living together before marriage?"

"They know we love one another. They're not like a lot of people who would prefer that we live apart until we're married. I told them that if you ever walked back into my life, I wanted to find out what we had by living together, and they agreed." She looked toward the window. "They love you, too, Tyler."

"I know they do. I love them, as well. I think you and Ali got lucky when it comes to getting a good set of parents. They remind me so much of my own mom and dad."

"Then," she whispered, sliding her hand across his jaw, "when we're done with Ali and Ram's call, I want you to come home with me and stay the night—and every night after that. Consider that an invitation you can't refuse!" She knew she was being bold, but nearly losing her life had taught her that some risks were worth taking. She saw the pleasure come to Tyler's eyes.

"I'm coming home with you until—or if— you ever kick me out."

"That will *never* happen," she whispered, closing her eyes, feeling his moist breath against her cheek. She lifted her chin, wanting nothing else but his mouth upon hers. Their kiss was searching and tender and she felt deep warmth grow in her belly as she lifted her hand and slid it across his broad shoulder. As she sank against Tyler, her breasts resting against his jacket, she felt him tense momentarily. There was such hunger in his kiss, and yet he restrained himself, allowing her to guide them where she desired. Her lips were a promise of what lay between them in so many ways, and she knew that Tyler got her message loud and clear about what kind of relationship she wanted with him.

Cara heard the phone in the living room ring and reluctantly broke the kiss, giving him a look of apology.

"Come on," he coaxed, standing. "Let's go inside. This is a happy occasion."

And it was, in every possible way. Cara tasted Tyler on her lower lip as she pulled out of his embrace. Shakily, they both stood, and Tyler offered her his hand. He was especially handsome tonight, looking more like a businessman than an ex-SEAL. Maybe that was what undercover work required—being a chameleon of sorts, adapting to whatever the situation demanded of him. But with her, he was always himself. When the three of them got finished talking with Ali and Ram, he knew that Cara was looking forward to him coming home with her. And if she had her way about it, it would be forever.

THERE WAS A lemon-colored slice of moon hanging in the dark Sonoran Desert night sky, the stars strewn like glittering gemstones tossed across the vault. Tyler spotted the constellation of Orion mid-heaven in its path across the heavens tonight. They parked their cars on a concrete slab, the garage doors closed. Cara explained they had to be opened by hand, but she was going to hire a man to install automatic garage door openers. Looking around, all he could see were patches of creosote brush, the saguaro cacti like dark, tall silhouettes here and there, and gravel and sand surrounding the home.

The house was typical of adobe homes—they looked like square blocks built on one floor, or on several. The roof was made of red tiles, with ten Palo Verde trees planted on the east and west sides of the home. He was sure someone had placed them there as shade protection against the rising and setting sun. In the summer, it could be a hundred degrees or more, and any shade would also cool the home.

It was a well thought out home, but Tyler was also looking at it from a black-ops perspective. The dirt road was two miles long, leading out into the flat desert floor. There were no homes nearby that he could see. Strategically, Cara had chosen well because from the house, he could see a vehicle coming from over a mile away. And the desert spread to the darkened horizon in every other direction.

"Do you like being out here alone like this?" he asked, following her to the front door, where she unlocked it.

"Definitely! I wanted the peace and quiet of nature, not the sound of traffic nearby."

"Ali is the same way," he said, pushing the door open for her after she opened it. "You do know that Ali and Ram just bought a house in Virginia?"

"Yes, but they're willing to sell it and come out here, from what she told me on the phone earlier." She turned on the lights.

Tyler shut the door. This was a new home with an open concept kitchen, dining room, and living room. Thick golden logs graced the ceiling, typical of this kind of adobe structure. "It's beautiful," he said, coming to her side. "Like you."

"Thanks." She gestured to the furniture in the living room. "I wanted a home that invited people to sit down and relax."

"It does that," he agreed.

She placed her purse in the foyer, inside a closet near the door, hanging the strap over a hook and shutting it. "Come, let me show you the master bathroom and bedroom." She slid her hand into his, and the look of longing he gave her made her dissolve with yearning.

He walked with her into the rear bedroom. The door was carved in dark-brown wood and he recognized Diego's crafting skills. There was a rising sun, several saguaros and a Harris hawk landing on top of one, the Sonoran Desert spreading out around the scene. He touched the wood, cool and polished to his touch. "Your papa has been here," he said, slanting a glance down at her, seeing the pride in her eyes.

"Papa insisted that every door in my home have one of his carvings. He is buying the doors and this was his first. Right now, he's working on the front door." Her voice lowered with affection. "He said this way, he and Mama are here in spirit, because he made them. I was so touched by that love and thoughtfulness."

"This is such a gift," Tyler said, admiring the man's artistry. Diego had no academic art schooling, yet, in his spare time—which wasn't much—he was doing this for his daughter. He was one hell of a father.

"We have talked over what I'd like to see on each door." She moved to the door, sliding her fingers over the Harris hawk. "I see these beautiful hawks everywhere in the desert. I found out a week after I moved in that there is a family of them less than half a mile from the house."

"Incredible."

"Come in," she urged, turning the brass knob and opening it.

Tyler followed her. He wanted to make long, slow love to this woman as he watched how gracefully she walked into the room. There were gossamer curtains across one window with dark lavender drapes at either end. A cream-colored carpet, nubby beneath his shoes, silenced their footsteps. There was a king-size bed with a brass headboard and footboard. He recognized a huge purple, cream, and soft-blue knit bedspread across it.

"Did you knit this?" he asked, running his hand across the soft angora yarn.

"I did. Do you like it?"

"It's soft, like you," he replied, turning her toward him, sliding his hands around her shoulders, and coaxing her into his arms, her lithe body resting against the front of him. He framed her face, looking deep into her sparkling eyes. "I want to love you, Cara. Is that what you want?"

"Oh, yes," she said, smiling shyly. "But first, let's shower, okay?"

"Absolutely." He released her, seeing the burning in her own eyes, feeling the imprint of her body against his. He wanted so much more with her. "Why don't you use the master bath. Do you have another bathroom?"

"Yes, in the second bedroom at the other end of the hall." She gave him a curious look. "You brought a suitcase. Do you have some pajamas in it?"

"I'm not going to wear them tonight."

Laughing, Cara said, "I expected that!" She leaned up and kissed his mouth. "We'll meet here after you've bathed."

CHAPTER 10

CARA'S HEART BEAT in a staccato of longing as Tyler led her to the edge of the bed, wearing only a white towel wrapped around his waist. For the first time, she could view his hard, tight, masculine body. She loved the dusting of black hair on his chest and lower arms. It turned her on even more, and the heat between them rose and crackled.

Cara breathed in the scent of sage soap as Tyler knelt down before her, an intense look on his handsome face that made her ache for him. He lifted his hands and opened the button of the pink silk trousers at her waist, then cupped her hips. As he slowly pulled the material down her curved thighs, he rasped, "Sit down on the bed, Cara."

She felt slightly dizzy as he held the material in place so she could sit comfortably on the mattress. She was now partly naked and could feel his hunger mounting for her. But Tyler wasn't in any hurry, his hands caressing her slender legs as he eased the silk off each of her limbs, setting the material aside. When he leaned over and caressed one foot, then the next, her skin tingled with zings of fire as he slowly skimmed her thighs. Then he moved back to her feet, as if memorizing—no, worshipping—her body.

He sat up, leaning against his heels, and pulled one of her feet up on his towel-covered thigh. The light was minimal in the room and Tyler reminded her of a powerful jaguar, even at rest, always alert. His long, rough fingers moved across each of her delicate toes and she saw him smile, his head bent as he began to massage each toe on her right foot. "Why are you smiling?" she asked him, her voice catching as he aroused her.

"I'm looking at your red toenail polish," he said, meeting her curious gaze.

"I've always painted my nails," she said, laughing.

Shaking his head, Tyler rasped, "I always wanted to see you like this," he admitted, now serious. "I swore if I got another chance, I was going to take my time loving you. Is that okay with you?"

More than okay. "You're really surprising me," she managed hoarsely, and then moaned as he expertly moved his thumb and forefinger around each of her toes, gently massaging each one. The sensations were delicious and completely unexpected.

"Do you like what I'm doing, sweetheart?"

Moaning, she whispered, "Oh, yes, that feels so good, Tyler. Ohhh, that feels wonderful. By the end of the day at school, my feet are aching. This is heavenly."

"Well, you won't have to worry about that again," he promised. "I'm sorry we had to be apart for nearly two months," he added, working on her delicate toes and graceful feet—slender, like the rest of her. Now, he placed her other foot on his thigh and began the same ritual of massaging each of her delicate toes, then her arch and heel.

"Mmmm," she whimpered, closing her eyes. "I've never had a man love me like this before . . ."

It made him feel wonderful to give back to her. Cara's belief that he was a good man gave him hope that he could please her fully. He'd had almost two months to put his broken marriage to rest within himself. Now, he was starting his life all over again. It hadn't been as hard to do as he'd first thought. Maybe his grief had finally dissolved, leaving the past where it belonged. But there wasn't a night that went by that he didn't dream of physically cherishing Cara.

At last, his heart was fully engaged, and touching her now was different from the way he had dreamed it would be. Her skin was firm and satiny beneath his exploring hands, and he plumbed her depths beyond just the physical. He allowed her sighs, her moans of appreciation, to fully enter his heart and take root there. These new feelings warmed him as never before, welling up into a newfound joy.

Cara was his miracle, bringing his desire for rebirth to them both.

Sliding his hands up her deliciously curved thighs, he leaned over and kissed her round belly, hearing her give a swift intake of breath. Her honey scent was overpowering as he licked her voluptuous skin with his tongue, feeling her begin to breathe more heavily as she opened herself even more to him, wanting to be taken by him even as he continued to seduce her. Someday, they both knew that she would carry his baby. The thought overwhelmed him, and he ached for the time when he would father their child.

Tyler savored her curved thighs that surrounded him in their warm, velvet embrace. He was determined to make Cara first in his life from now on. All he wanted was to pleasure her, hear these sweet sounds rising in her throat, watch her nipples contract and harden beneath that silken material as she begged to be touched at her deepest core.

"Lie back on the bed," he rasped, staring deep into her glazed eyes. Tyler heard her quickened breaths and saw the growing need for him in her eyes, begging for culmination. He arranged her so she lay fully on her back, then eased onto the bed and straddled her, his knees bracketing her full hips. His towel fell away and he dropped it on the floor. Slowly, he pulled the thin straps of her gossamer top off her shoulders, and was dazzled by the perfection of her small, perfect breasts, the nipples so tight that they lured him to them, begging to be touched.

Tyler grasped her hands, guiding them above her head as he held her gaze, his erection rock hard against the warm softness of her abdomen. Leaning down, he captured one of her rosy nipples, sucking gently on it, her moan vibrating through him as he gave her more pleasure. He wanted Cara soaking wet and ready to receive him. Her eyes were closed as he lifted his mouth away from the nipple, observing the growing tension and excitement on her face. He kept her wrists crossing each other, lightly held in place with one of his hands in case she wanted to free herself. When he licked her other nipple, Cara's hips instantly lifted in response. He couldn't hold back his groan as his erection was trapped between the slick dampness of their bodies. Slowly, he began to thrust against her, feeling the sleek velvet of her body against him, glorying in the sensations as he continued to focus on her nipples.

He wasn't surprised when she tried to open her thighs to him, silently asking him to enter her.

"Not yet, Cara, not yet," he crooned, easing forward, nipping her slender neck, hearing the protest that vibrated in her exposed throat. The trust Cara gave him, the surrender of her heart and body to him, touched him so deeply that his eyes burned with unshed tears. Tyler wanted to worship her forever. Lifting his head, he crushed his mouth against hers, feeling her fuse with him, her hunger for consummation equal to his. He hardened even more—if that was possible—and he almost considered climaxing outside of her. Strangling that desire with steely control, he took her willing mouth, sliding his lips against hers, feeling her smile beneath his, relishing her enjoyment of all he was sharing with her.

Easing from her wet, hungry lips, he lifted his leg, releasing her hands and kneeling between her spreading thighs. Brushing his fingers lightly against her core, his fingers instantly became soaked. She was so turned on, so *ripe*, so ready for him.

Leaning across her, Tyler placed his erection against her entrance, slowly rubbing against her, teasing her. She instantly reacted, groaning his name, her hands settling around his narrow hips, trying to pull him forward, trying to get him inside her. He placed his elbows near Cara's shoulders, his hands framing her flushed face, drowning in the glistening gold-brown diamonds reflected in her luminous eyes. She was such a sensual creature, and he could feel her primal challenge to him as she lifted her hips, grazing him, making him groan with her wetness as she teased him in return.

Gritting his teeth, he nudged himself into her, watching her eyes grow cloudy with urgency, her pleading whimpers tearing from her parted lips. She felt like a hot, tight, wet glove beginning to envelop him. Tyler wasn't going to tease her, instead, he wanted to slowly open her, get her to widen and accept his thick length. First, her body needed to relax, instead of clenching against him as he slowly thrust another inch into her.

Then, Cara choked and froze.

"Am I hurting you?" he demanded, his voice a rasp.

"It's . . . it's . . . uncomfortable," she managed. "Give me some time so my body can adjust to you, okay?"

Pressing his sweaty brow against hers, both of them breathing rapidly, he urged, "Take it easy, sweetheart. We have time. Just relax, and tell me when it's okay to move . . ."

How much he enjoyed talking with her, pleasing her first, not second. It didn't take long before Cara lifted her hips, giving him the silent signal.

Tyler felt her walls around him slowly relax and welcome him, the fluids slick and plentiful. He leaned down, sampling one of her nipples. She cried out, panting, her fingers digging frantically into his shoulders. Her body contracted and he could feel her getting ready to climax. Gently, he began a slow, pleasurable rhythm, slipping a little deeper into her warm, willing body. Each time she whimpered, calling his name, wanting more of him inside her.

When he was fully engaged, Tyler knew exactly where those super-sensitive nerves could be found. Cara's breathing became shallower as he pulled one of her nipples into his mouth, suckling her hard and feeling her buck, arching her back and crying out as he urged that jagged fire that would explode through her boiling lower body.

At the same time, he began short, hard strokes to trigger that cloister of nerves. Her cries heightened, Cara sobbing his name as she tightened around him. In moments, her hands grasped his shoulders as her lower body jerked, back bowing, her orgasm overwhelming her. Lovingly, he stroked her, allowing her all the time she wanted to enjoy the intensity of her orgasm as it rippled through her lower body.

Minutes later, exhausted, Cara barely opened her eyes. Tyler's erection was thick, throbbing, and she could feel him holding himself back, trying not to come. Weakly, she lifted her legs, wrapping them around his narrow, taut hips, pulling him as deeply as he could go inside her. He filled and widened her, making her feel like an opulent sexual creature—female in ways she had never experienced before this.

How she savored his strength, his power as a man! She luxuriated in the gifts he continued to bestow upon her. Her hips now thrust against his, tearing a primal growl from him, his fists bunching into the covers on either side of her head. Another vibrating growl tore out of him. He stiffened, surging his hips against hers, fusing with her, and she felt his hot release as he whimpered with ongoing pleasure.

Tyler collapsed against her afterward, his head resting against hers, breathing harshly, sweat running down his face. Cara smiled weakly, enclosing him with her arms, needing this, needing him. Nothing had ever felt so right as this very moment with Tyler covering her, his weight like a heavy, warm blanket against her panting, wet body. Their sweat mingled and small rivulets combined, trickling down across her skin.

Cara leaned over him, her lips claiming his, tasting him as he reclaimed her mouth urgently, thrusting his tongue into hers, making her moan. He threaded his fingers through her long, black hair, drawing her to him, hungry again and demanding access to her swollen lips.

She sighed with pleasure, so exhausted she could barely move. She lay there, wrapped in wonder, grateful for this man in her life.

Tyler finally moved. Looking down at her, he said, "You're so sexy and beautiful." He kissed her smooth brow, her cheek, her nose and finally, grazed her lips. He levered himself up so they remained melded at the hips, most of his weight off her. Then, slowly, he pulled out of her. He looked at her with the deepest love he had ever felt, and she gave him a soft smile, her hands sliding down his arms, accepting him completely, and making a humming sound of utter satisfaction as he removed himself from her.

"I love you, Tyler Hutton," she whispered, her voice low and filled with emotion. "You are incredible . . . I feel so satisfied, and all I can say is, thank you . . ."

Her husky words sank into his thudding heart. "I love you more than life, Cara. Now come close and lie on your side with me. We need to sleep in one another's arms." He brought her against him, wrapping his larger body in a curve around her smaller one, her head coming to rest on his shoulder, drifting towards sleep.

They had just made an incredible breakthrough, escalating their already serious relationship. Kissing her silky hair, smoothing his knuckles down her flushed cheek, he watched her slide into the folds of sleep. When her body sank against his, her lashes closed, her breathing grew shallow, and he knew she was sleeping.

His heart felt as if it were going to explode—right now, he felt more joyous emotions than he'd ever experienced at one time. Cara had given him a second chance, and now, she was his. *Forever.*

CARA AWOKE SLOWLY, barely able to open her eyes. She laid on her side, curved against Tyler's larger body, his arm across her waist, holding her close even as he slept. There was a clock on the bed-stand that read five a.m. She had another hour before she had to get up and get ready for work.

"You awake?"

She smiled a little, hearing Tyler's sleepy voice near her ear. "Yes. Just woke up."

He groaned, and then rose up on one elbow, staring at the clock.

"0500."

"I have to get up at six to get ready to go to work."

He sat up, rubbing his eyes. "Hmmm, we have an hour . . . good."

She turned onto her back, looking up at him. He was beautiful when naked, an incredible male specimen. There was no fat on his body, just pure, lean, hard muscle. "Why is that good?" She realized her own voice sounded husky with sleep.

He sat up, pulling up the covers to his waist, pushed his back against the headboard and reached into the bed-stand drawer. "Because," he said, "I have something I want to give to you. Come over here, sweetheart."

She scooted over to where he sat, snuggling beneath his left arm, resting her cheek against the warmth of his skin on his broad shoulder. "Oh?"

A boyish smile curved his mouth as he gave her a mischievous look. "First, give me your hand."

She offered her left hand and he slipped a red velvet box into it with the lid open. Gasping, she stared down at the set of wedding rings. Only, this wasn't a typical diamond set. There were small chocolate- and pink-colored diamonds on the engagement ring. The wedding ring was a simple solitaire pink sapphire surrounded by very small, chocolate-colored diamonds.

"This," she whispered, sitting up, the covers falling to her waist, "is so beautiful, Tyler!"

He slid his arm around her waist, watching her delight with the colors of the gemstones. "I know it may be too soon to ask you to marry me, Cara, but I wanted you to know that these rings are yours whenever you want to wear them."

"We haven't had a chance to live together, that's true," she said, touching the pink faceted sapphire lovingly with her fingertip.

"I don't want you to feel rushed." He shrugged a little. "This set promises you that I'm serious about you, about us, and my hopes for a very happy future together."

"It's a promise," she whispered, choking up, her eyes brimming with tears as she held his somber gaze. "I know we love one another. That's never been the question."

"I agree. But I'm concerned about what your parents might think if I didn't show you and them, my intentions toward you. I know Latinos are very tied to ceremony, and marriage is very important to them, and their family, as a whole."

She smiled a little. "You're right. I know my parents try to be modern, but we have some very old, good rules about marriage. I know they're okay with us living together, but I think you were very wise in giving these to me. I'll show them to Mama and Papa. I'm sure it will make them feel even better about us and our trial period of living together."

"That's what I thought."

She picked out the engagement ring. "But I want to wear this one, Tyler."

His brows moved upward. "Really? To reassure your parents about us?"

"No . . . nothing like that." She placed the ring in his hand. "You can slip it on my finger. I want to wear it because I know our living together is only going to make us happier and happier. I know we'll get married, but it should be at such a time that my parents feel comfortable with it. In our culture we have long engagements, a year or longer."

Chuckling, he said, "Hey, I'm fine with anything you want, sweetheart." He slid the ring on her slender finger, admiring the flashes of chocolate and pink as she moved her hand slightly, enjoying the glimmering colors. "My dad made this set of rings for you. I flew home for a weekend to see my folks and told them about you, about the dreams I had of marrying you some day. My dad asked me the color of your eyes, and then he asked what kind of woman you were. I told him you were all heart." His voice lowered. "He took me out to his gem office and pulled out this pink sapphire. He'd found this early on in his mining days and had held onto it because it was flawless as a faceted gemstone. When he asked me if I thought you might like the combination of chocolate diamonds and the pink sapphire, I told him I felt you'd love it." Lifting his head, he met and held her tearful gaze. "Was I right? Pink sapphires are pretty rare and this one is very large, which makes it even more rare."

"You were right." She reached out, grazing his cheeks, loving the way short strands of hair dipped across his brow. "When I saw the chocolate diamonds, I thought they were almost

212 | LINDSAY McKENNA

the exact color of my eyes."

"They are, but they have gold in their depths when you're happy, Cara." He caught her hand, kissing the back of it. "Or when we make love to one another . . ."

She sighed and rested her brow against his naked, warm shoulder. "This wedding set is so special because your father made it for me. I hope I can meet your parents soon."

"I figure, if you're open to it, Cara, we could fly up to Montana after school is over in early June. My parents are so excited about you. I had a photo of you and they thought you were beautiful."

She felt heat moving into her cheeks. "Maybe that would be a good time to talk about setting a wedding date, and get them in on the ground floor. Perhaps a mid-December wedding would work for them? I get a holiday break then, through the first week in January."

"Sounds good to me. Where would you like to go for a honeymoon?"

"I—well, I never thought about that before, Tyler . . . and it would cost so much money."

"That's something you don't have to worry about," he countered. "I make two-hundred and fifty-thousand dollars a year. We can afford to go to the place of your dreams."

Her eyes widened over the amount. "But where I want to go is so far away."

"The world is yours, Cara. All I want to do is make you happy and enjoy every hour of every day with you."

Wincing a little, she said, "Then, I'd love to visit Australia, but not just anywhere there. I want to go to the Red Center, to Uluru. I want to meet, talk, and be with Aboriginal people. Mama had me read a book about the bush people and I fell in love with them. These people are survivors, Tyler. They live in a harsh desert climate. I saw color plates of their cave drawings, just like Mama's people and their petroglyphs. When I was little, I loved drawing them. When I saw the Aboriginal petroglyphs in the book, they were similar to ours, and I got curious about why there would be such a crossover when we lived half a globe apart."

"Then," he said, "we'll go. We'll make it a two-week trip. As an operator, I worked out of Alice Springs in Australia on a couple of missions. That town is near Uluru. Let me research this more and we'll decide where we want to get a hotel. Then, you can make connections with the Aboriginal people because they live all around that area. How does that sound?"

She gave him a sudden grin, squeezing his hand. "Wonderful! I'm so excited! I never in my wildest imagination thought I'd get to Australia to visit these wonderful people!"

Tyler gathered her into his arms, placing the

jewelry box on the bed-stand. He cuddled her against him, feeling her soft, womanly warmth, drowning in her eyes shining with gold in their depths. He kissed her tousled black hair. "I can see that our life together will hold a thousand wonderful surprises, Cara. But you are definitely the best surprise of all. We're going to have a good life together. Forever."

END

Don't miss Lindsay McKenna's next book,
Christmas with my Cowboy
Available from Kensington!

Turn the page for a sneak peek of
Christmas with my Cowboy

Excerpt from

Christmas with my Cowboy
by Lindsay McKenna

T HE STUDIO WAS warming up. And Christmas was coming. Travis Grant checked the progress on each of his six projects. Thanks to Steve and Maud Whitcomb, owners of the Wind River Ranch, his career as a furniture maker had taken off. Steve was a world class architect, and he'd invited Architecture Magazine to send out a reporter to do a story on him last year. He'd had three pieces of furniture under way at that time, trying to make a living between being a wrangler on their ranch during the summer months, and the other eight months of winter, creating beautiful furniture. That one article catapulted him from being a nobody to a somebody in the world of high class, handmade furniture.

He was forever indebted to his bosses for their support. He and Maud had ordered and bought two pieces from him, already. The money was more than good and he'd been able to buy this small farm that sat along Route 89 near Wind

River, Wyoming. It only had five acres to it, a fifteen hundred square foot single story turn-of-the-century cabin on it, a two-story barn, corrals and a huge garden area. For him, it meant safety, solace and finding peace that eluded him since getting PTSD.

Seeing the flash of headlights through his double-paned window, he scowled. Who the hell was out at this time of morning and in these deadly weather conditions? The beams had turned in a three-hundred and sixty circle on Route 89. That meant someone had hit black ice and lost control.

Damn.

He pulled his black Stetson down a little tighter on his head, hauled on his thick elk skin gloves to protect his hands from the plummeting temperature and quickly headed out of the barn. The wind was hard, battering against his body as he ran to the garage. He hit the door opener and waited impatiently to get to his huge Chevy RAM three-quarter ton pickup inside. His dirt road was now muddy and iced, as well. Climbing in, he backed out, a sense of urgency filling him.

Probably some stupid tourist or a person who didn't really understand Wyoming blizzard weather could kill them, he thought as he drove slowly through the ice-covered mud ruts. They'd already gotten two feet of snow a week ago, and the plows had just finished pushing it off the sides of the highway. There was no way he could speed down his quarter mile driveway or he'd spin out, too. Mouth tightening, Travis saw that the car, a bright red one, had spun out and was now tipped on its side in the huge ditch next to the entrance of his property.

Travis parked and got out, seeing steam rising from beneath the hood. He couldn't see who was in the vehicle yet because of all the white airbags had deployed, but there was no movement. The windshield wipers on the car were still, indicating the car's engine was off. There was no movement inside the car yet and that bothered Travis. All he could see as he slipped and slid down the short slope of mud and snow, was the white deployed air bags. His mind automatically began to tick off potential medical issues. As a trained Recon Marine, Travis was more than knowledgeable about medical emergency situations, what to do and how to handle them.

The wind, sharp and cold, tore at him, his ears unprotected. Was the person in this car injured? Seeing no movement bothered him greatly now. As he reached the car door, he couldn't see the person, just their outline beneath the limp air bags that covered them. Eyes narrowing, he saw only one person in the car. Knocking on the window, the person didn't move. He called out to them. No answer. They could be unconscious. *Double damn.*

Travis didn't need this with a blue norther blizzard coming down hard on the area shortly. There was no way an ambulance would try to make it out here from the small hospital in Wind River, twenty miles away. The first responders knew better than to try and drive after the road had just been shut down by the sheriff's department, according to his weather radio an hour ago. This car and driver were probably the last to make it onto Route 89 before they closed it. No Wyoming person would ever go out in this kind of killing weather.

He yanked open the door. It grudgingly gave way.

"Hey," Travis called, pushing the white air bag out of the way. "Are you all right?"

His heart crashed in his chest.

There, lying unconscious, slumped in her seat belt, was Kassie Murphy!

His mind blanked out briefly as he froze, so many blips from their past talks, kissing her, leaving her, slammed through him. Travis shook himself out of his state, reaching in after yanking off a glove, his two fingers pressed gently against the side of her slender neck, searching for a pulse. Her black hair, thick and luxurious, had swirled around her shoulders, covering part of her face. Worse, as he felt for a pulse against her carotid artery, he saw just how pale she'd become. And then, as he swiftly perused her for other injury, he saw a thin trail of blood leaking out from beneath her hairline along her left temple.

Kass! No! No, this couldn't be happening!

Travis felt as if his whole, carefully structured life since returning to civilian life a year ago, had just been shattered. The woman he loved was right here in front of him. Unconscious. Injured. And he'd left her a year ago, telling her they'd never make it in a relationship because of the severity of his PTSD. He released her, wanting her to have a chance at real love with a normal man, not someone as shattered inwardly as he was. Kass had cried that day as they'd had that gut-wrenching conversation. Her tears felt like acid eating away what was left of his heart. He loved her enough to release her. There was no way he was going to accidentally injure her by living with him. It just wouldn't work.

His heart leapt in his chest. A pulse! There! It was strong and constant. That was a good sign.

Swallowing hard, tears jamming into his eyes, Travis fought them back. He heard her moan, her parted lips closing for a moment as she began to become conscious.

"Kass? It's Travis. Stay still, you've been in a car accident. I'm going to unsnap your seat belt and get you out of here. Just hold on . . . ."

The Books of Delos

Title: ***Last Chance*** (Prologue)
Publish Date: July 15, 2015
Learn more at:
delos.lindsaymckenna.com/last-chance

Title: ***Nowhere to Hide***
Publish Date: October 13, 2015
Learn more at:
delos.lindsaymckenna.com/nowhere-to-hide

Title: ***Tangled Pursuit***
Publish Date: November 11, 2015
Learn more at:
delos.lindsaymckenna.com/tangled-pursuit

Title: ***Forged in Fire***
Publish Date: December 3, 2015
Learn more at:
delos.lindsaymckenna.com/forged-in-fire

Title: ***Broken Dreams***
Publish Date: January 2, 2016
Learn more at:
delos.lindsaymckenna.com/broken-dreams

Title: ***Blind Sided***
Publish Date: June 5, 2016
Learn more at:
delos.lindsaymckenna.com/blind-sided

Title: ***Secret Dream***
Publish Date: July 25, 2016
Learn more at:
delos.lindsaymckenna.com/secret-dream

Title: ***Hold On***
Publish Date: August 3, 2016
Learn more at:
delos.lindsaymckenna.com/hold-on

Title: ***Hold Me***
Publish Date: August 11, 2016
Learn more at
delos.lindsaymckenna.com/hold-me

Title: ***Unbound Pursuit***
Publish Date: September 29, 2016
Learn more at:
delos.lindsaymckenna.com/unbound-pursuit

Title: ***Secrets***
Publish Date: November 21, 2016
Learn more at:
delos.lindsaymckenna.com/secrets

Title: ***Snowflake's Gift***
Publish Date: February 4, 2017
Learn more at:
delos.lindsaymckenna.com/snowflakes-gift

Title: ***Never Enough***
Publish Date: March 1, 2017
Learn more at:
delos.lindsaymckenna.com/never-enough

Title: ***Dream of Me***
Publish Date: May 23, 2017
Learn more at:
delos.lindsaymckenna.com/dream-of-me

Title: ***Trapped***
Publish Date: July 17, 2017
Learn more at:
delos.lindsaymckenna.com/trapped

Title: ***Taking A Chance***
Publish Date: August 1, 2017
Learn more at:
delos.lindsaymckenna.com/taking-a-chance

Everything Delos!

Newsletter

Please visit my newsletter website at newsletter.lindsaymckenna.com. The newsletter will have exclusive information about my books, publishing schedule, giveaways, exclusive cover peeks, and more.

Delos Series Website

Be sure to drop by my website dedicated to the Delos Series at delos.lindsaymckenna.com. There will be new articles on characters, my publishing schedule, and information about each book written by Lindsay.

Made in the USA
Middletown, DE
14 December 2023